CROSSING THE LINE

THE BALTIMORE BANNERS (BOOK 1)

LISA B. KAMPS

CROSSING THE LINE

LISA B. KAMPS

CROSSING THE LINE

CROSSING THE LINE
Copyright © 2015 by Elizabeth Belbot Kamps

All rights reserved. Except for use in any review, the reproduction or utilization of this work in whole or in part in any form by any electronic, mechanical or other means, now known or hereafter invented, including xerography, photocopying and recording, or in any information storage or retrieval system, is forbidden without the express written permission of the author.
The Baltimore Banners© is a fictional professional ice hockey team, created for the sole use of the author and covered under protection of copyright.
All characters in this book have no existence outside the imagination of the author and have no relation to anyone bearing the same name or names, living or dead. This book is a work of fiction and any resemblance to any individual, place, business, or event is purely coincidental.

Cover design by Jay Aheer of Simply Defined Art
http://www.jayscoversbydesign.com/

LISA B. KAMPS

All rights reserved.
ISBN: 1514737426
ISBN-13: 978-1514737422

CONTENTS

Copyright	v
Dedication	11
Other titles by this author	13
ONE	15
TWO	24
THREE	31
FOUR	40
FIVE	51
SIX	59
SEVEN	68
EIGHT	77
NINE	88
TEN	95
TWELVE	113
THIRTEEN	122
FOURTEEN	130
FIFTEEN	137
SIXTEEN	148
SEVENTEEN	156
EIGHTEEN	169
NINETEEN	177
About the Author	185

For Scott Lloyd...boss, (tor)mentor, confidant, best friend.

Your craziness, your support, and your brutal honestly made sure I kept the dream alive! For that, I can never repay you. Well, okay, I know a few lattes and some chicken tikka masala won't hurt...!

Other titles by this author

Emeralds and Gold: A Treasury of Irish Short Stories *(anthology)*

Finding Dr. Right, Silhouette Special Edition

Crossing The Line (The Baltimore Banners, Book 1)

Game Over (The Baltimore Banners, Book 2)

Blue Ribbon Summer (The Baltimore Banners, Book 3)

ONE

"There's no way, AJ. Impossible."

Amber Johnson eyed her editor, Tim Norton, so confident and relaxed behind the littered desk, and suppressed the urge to slug him.

"Not impossible. I'm as qualified as anyone and you know it. You can at least give me a chance." Her words were rushed, not quite hiding the desperation she felt at his announcement. She *was* qualified, and Tim knew it.

"AJ, this isn't some human interest story or a piece of feel-good fluff that you're used to—"

"I'm capable of a lot more."

Tim tapped his pencil against a bare spot on his desk, the rapid tap-tap-tap threatening to launch one of her rare but lethal migraines. She clenched her back teeth but didn't say anything. Tim's pencil-tapping was a sign that he was contemplating. What, she didn't know, but she wanted this bad enough that she was willing to wait for whatever was going on inside his balding blonde head.

The annoying tapping finally stopped and he looked her over, starting at the bare toes peeking out from her leather sandals and working his way up her low-rise denim capris. His gaze stopped on the cut of her scoop neck shirt longer than necessary before his eyes finally met hers.

"AJ, you don't even look the part. Lord knows I have guys around here that are just as qualified and fit the image better than you."

She crossed her arms, hiding the neckline of her shirt and trying to reign in her anger. It bubbled beneath her breastbone, a heated sensation that burned all the way to her stomach. But before she could even open her mouth with a comeback—not that she had one—Tim stood up and walked over to his office door, closing it with a loud click.

"But..." He returned to his worn chair and lowered himself into it. "You have talent. I told you that a while ago. And I like your writing style. So..."

AJ relaxed the grip she had on her arms and held her breath, afraid to even blink in case she missed whatever Tim was about to say.

"I'll make you a deal. Do one story that blows me away, and you'll be in the running."

The brief glimmer she felt just a minute before quickly died. "In the running? That's it?"

"Don't get all indignant with me. The running isn't that broad."

Tim didn't elaborate. AJ slowly lowered her arms and studied him, not sure what to expect. Her guard went up just a bit. "How broad?"

A few seconds of silence went by before Tim let his breath out in a long weary sigh. "Counting you, two. Maybe three. No, probably just two."

Two, counting her. Excitement tingled along AJ's spine, warming her. Her chances were fifty-fifty of getting the job. Maybe even better than that, depending on who else Tim was considering. Some of her excitement died when she realized who Tim would consider the obvious choice.

"And don't say a word!" Tim wagged a finger in her direction and she snapped her mouth closed, biting back the comment she was going to make. "He's good at what he does and he pulls the readers in, which is good for our circulation."

AJ honestly didn't think the circulation would be hurt one bit if *he* disappeared off the face of the earth but she knew better than to say so. This time, anyway.

He was Gerry Brown, the self-proclaimed god of sports journalism. As far as the female staff was concerned, he might as well be the god of athlete's foot. Tall and lean with a square face and dimples-on-demand, Gerry Brown thought of himself as Number One—an opinion he shared with others but that others rarely shared with him. The downside was that despite his shortcomings, he really could write. "The asshole."

"AJ..."

"Oops. Did I say that out loud?" She looked over at Tim with wide eyes and an innocent face. He snorted in a cross between amusement and exasperation then shook his head.

"AJ, if you're serious about this job, you need to stop stuff like that. Your writing is strong and your style is unique. It's your mouth that gets you in trouble. Why I'm even thinking about offering you a chance..."

"But you did." AJ straightened, serious now. Tim was right, her mouth *did* get her into trouble. "One story, right? So how do you want me to handle this? I go find someone then come up with something—"

"Not quite. I have a very specific assignment in mind." Tim pushed through the piles on his desk, his brow wrinkled as he pulled on a tattered post-it and studied it. "Here it is."

AJ didn't even bother to ask. Tim had these moments every once in awhile where he disappeared into his own mind, retrieving some important bit of information. How the man kept track of anything was beyond her. Personally if she didn't write it down herself, chances were it either didn't get done or else it got forgotten.

"They want to try something new around here, something a little different. I don't even bother to question anymore, just go with it. So here it is. Go see what you can come up with."

AJ took the tattered post-it from Tim's outstretched hand then glanced down at it. The bottom dropped from her stomach when she saw the name scrawled across the wrinkled surface. "You're joking, right? This is impossible."

"No joke, and not my idea. Come up with something."

"But he doesn't do interviews!"

"Be creative, but come up with something."

"Tim—"

"AJ, look at you." His hands motioned in her direction, wildly moving up and down. "He's a guy. I'm sure you can come up with something to get him to change his mind."

"Hey! Are you suggesting—"

"I'm not suggesting anything, just being realistic. Look at it this way: at least you have one advantage you can use over Gerry."

"He's doing the same assignment?"

"Yup."

AJ fell silent. There was no way this could work out. She glanced down at the name on the paper again and blew out a deep breath. Why him, of all people?

Alec Kolchak, super-star goalie of the Baltimore Banners. Probably the best goalie in the NHL. And quite possibly the most private athlete in the sports world. Alec Kolchak did not do interviews, period. Everyone knew that.

And even if he did, the chances of him ever talking to her were so low it was almost laughable. Almost.

AJ inhaled deeply then let her breath out in a rush. She wanted to slug something at the gross unfairness of it all. Her one shot, and it was impossible.

Maybe.

Then again, maybe not.

She muttered a hasty goodbye to Tim and walked out of his office, not even paying attention to his last words. Her mind was working already, coming up with ideas and tactics. Maybe Tim was right when he suggested being creative. Maybe she could come up with something...

It didn't matter if it worked or not. In fact, AJ was honest enough with herself to know it probably wouldn't. But she couldn't give it up without at least trying.

#

Alec paused a few feet from his truck and nearly dropped the gym bag in his hand at the sight in front of him.

It had been nearly two years, yet he felt the familiar irritation—and unwelcome attraction—flood him as if only a few days had gone by. He clenched his jaw and bit back the retort that sprang to mind, refusing to get drawn into the old battle. Determined to ignore her, he reached out for the door handle but stopped when she moved directly in front of him.

"Hey Alec. Long time, no see."

The hesitant greeting only made him roll his eyes and look behind him, to see if any of his teammates were nearby to run interference for him. The lot was inconveniently empty.

Sighing, Alec turned back toward his truck and looked down, then immediately wished he hadn't. His gaze shifted too far south and he found himself staring at a large expanse of smooth, round, tan skin.

"For crying out loud, AJ, why don't you go put on some decent clothes? There are kids around in case you hadn't noticed!" His outburst surprised him as much as it obviously did her, and he bit his tongue too late at the forlorn expression that spread across her face. He almost apologized until he noticed her stubborn chin lift a few inches in defiance.

"There's nothing wrong with this shirt! And if you have a problem with it then you should stop staring!"

Alec realized she was right, he *was* staring. Muttering under his breath, he reached around her and pulled open the door, ignoring the heat of her skin as his arm brushed across her shoulder. He chalked his body's reaction up to too much stress lately. It certainly did *not* have anything to do with the girl standing in front of him.

Amber "AJ" Johnson was nothing more than an annoyance, and always had been. It didn't matter that nearly two years had passed since he had seen her; she was still the same annoying girl who had always bugged everyone on the team under the pretense of writing one article or another for a local sports tabloid.

Except she didn't exactly look the same. Her hair was longer and straighter than he remembered, and not quite as dark. There were lighter streaks running through the strands framing her oval face, making her blue eyes appear wider.

Or maybe they looked wider because she was staring at him in frustration. Probably because he was still staring at her. Her faded jeans were tight, stopping just below her knees and clinging to curves he didn't remember her having. At least Alec knew why she seemed taller than before: she was wearing a pair of strappy sandals with a three-inch heel that showed off tanned feet and polished nails. And that shirt...the shirt, if you could even call it that, had to go. Alec guessed it was supposed to be some kind of tank shirt but the straps were barely wide enough to hold it up, and the front was cut so deep he wondered if she had it on backwards.

"What is your problem, Kolchak? You're acting like you've never seen a girl before!"

AJ's sarcastic comment was enough to snap him out of whatever mental fog he had lapsed into. His eyes narrowed and he expected her to move out of his way so he could climb into the truck. He wasn't surprised when she didn't, so he brushed by her, gently nudging her out of his way.

"Don't lean against my truck, you're going to scratch the paint." Alec jumped inside and slammed the door before she could make any other comment and quickly started the engine before throwing the truck in gear, needing to get home and away from the sudden madness that threatened him.

And it was madness. That was the only explanation he could think of for his startling reaction to seeing her again.

#

AJ wondered why she was even bothering.

The computer screen stared back at her, silently accusing. Or maybe that was blankly accusing, she thought, since that's exactly what she was looking at: a blank screen.

She had spent the entire day searching for information on Alec Kolchak but found absolutely nothing she didn't already know. In fact, AJ was beginning to realize that she actually knew more than what was actually floating around in cyberspace, just based on her casual association with him and other members of the team a few years ago. But none of it was stuff she could use.

Alec Kolchak was one of the best goalies in the NHL, and the only things she could find on him were his stats: where he was born, when he was drafted, his game stats. Most of that information came directly from the Banners' very own website.

Because Alec Kolchak did not do interviews. Period.

She was insane to think he would ever agree to do one with her.

AJ inhaled deeply then let her breath out in a rush. She wanted to slug something at the gross unfairness of it all. Her one shot, and it was impossible.

She blew the hair out of her eyes, minimized the word processor screen, then rolled her mouse over the desktop icons, double-clicking on the one for a card game. It was a waste of time but AJ started it anyway. It was better than staring at a blank screen, and required absolutely no thought whatsoever.

Guilt crept over her after five minutes of mindless playing and she quit the game, not able to get any enjoyment out of it. Not that she was enjoying the still-blank screen of the word processor, either.

With a grunt of frustration, AJ closed out the program and pushed away from her desk, muttering to herself. One of the reasons she was having such trouble writing anything was because she didn't have anything to write that people didn't already know. That didn't mean she was ready to give up, not if she was seriously considering going after this job.

And she *was* serious. Too bad for her that it was going to be almost impossible. The only bright side was that she had heard through the grapevine that Gerry Brown had an even worse experience when he first tried speaking to Kolchak. Rumor got back to her that he was asked to leave the rink and that one of the rookies had actually locked the door when Gerry tried to get back in.

At least she had actually talked with Alec. Kind of. A little. Maybe. The whole meeting still left her a bit dazed. Because really, what was that bit with the whole shirt? It still made no sense. And then for him to tell her she was going to scratch the paint on his truck.

The jerk.

AJ threaded her way down the hall to her small bedroom and rummaged through her closet. She yanked a scoop neck tank from a hanger then quickly changed, throwing a short-sleeve shirt over top. She thought about buttoning the shirt, then changed her mind and left it hanging open, deciding to use what she had to her advantage. Although, from Alec's reaction yesterday, maybe it wasn't an advantage.

"Yeah, well, if it works..." The sound of her voice made her wince and she wondered if she was caving into unseen pressure. Shrugging off the thought, AJ grabbed her car keys and left the apartment. She had just enough time to reach the arena to make a pest of herself prior to the game. And if that didn't work, she planned on staying to watch, then making a pest of herself after the game. And who knew? With her carefully chosen ticket, she might even be a nuisance during the game. At this point she doubted if it could hurt any.

#

Alec took a quick drink of water from the bottle resting on the back of the net then breathed deeply, trying to keep his focus on center ice. With any luck, this would be the last face-off of the game and the Banners would win again. With any luck…

So far his luck had been holding out. Barely. The puck had crossed into the net behind him twice tonight, but they had both been hard shots. It didn't make him feel great, but at least they weren't shots that he *should* have stopped, like in the last few games. He could be thankful for that.

All he had to do was keep his attention focused on the game and not worry about the girl seated right behind the glass to his left.

That should have been easy to do. Easier than breathing. But for some reason his attention kept drifting and that bothered him. He didn't need the distraction. He was better at keeping himself focused…usually.

The girl in question was standing, her attention on center ice—along with all the other fans here for tonight's game. She had shown up earlier in another pair of too-tight jeans and low-cut shirt, but at least she had been wearing a worn-out denim jacket that had seen better days. Not that *that* had stopped some of the players from ogling her. Alec had been tempted to go up to her when she was standing by the players' entrance and read her the riot act for dressing like that.

Didn't she know the players had to concentrate before a game? That they didn't need distractions when they were supposed to be getting ready? Not that any of the players seemed to mind, which irritated Alec even more for a reason he didn't understand.

He glanced over to the stands and gritted his teeth. Her denim jacket was gone now, which he didn't really understand. Despite being mid-Fall, summer weather was hanging on in Baltimore, but it was still chilly in the arena. She had to be cold, with pretty much her entire upper body exposed like that. What was she thinking, dressing like that…

Alec's attention shot to center ice at the sound of the puck dropping and all thoughts of AJ Johnson disappeared from his mind. His eyes followed the spot of black, his breathing slow as he watched sticks fight for control of it. The hard piece of rubber came sliding toward him at warp speed and he crouched low, ready for it, only to have one of his teammates slap it away from him. The puck careened across the ice, crossing the center line and entering the offensive zone, and Alec relaxed his stance. He glanced up at the clock and saw the seconds ticking by...four, three, two...

The horn sounded, signaling the end of the game, and Alec breathed a deep sigh of relief. The Banners won! Maybe his slump was finally over.

He looked to his left and noticed AJ watching him, a broad smile lighting her face. She caught his eye and nodded at him, almost as if she was saying "Good job". He caught himself smiling back at her before he could stop himself. As soon as he realized what he was doing, he frowned and looked away, then skated out of the net to meet his teammates. He grunted under their well-meant claps of congratulations and mild-mannered barbs, refusing to think about the look of disappointment he could have sworn crossed AJ's face when he frowned at her.

TWO

"What are you doing here, Johnson?"

AJ tensed at the clipped words coming from behind her and bit her tongue. It was so tempting to turn around and fire back with a sarcastic comment, but hardly worth the effort. Number one, the comment would be lost on the speaker. Number two, she needed to focus on her plan.

She took a deep breath, held it to the count of five, then slowly turned and eyed Gerry Brown with all the cool disdain she could muster. Not that he noticed—he was too busy slicking back his hair and smoothing his shirt sleeves to pay any attention.

"I'm waiting. What are *you* doing here?"

He finally looked at her, his pale brows drawn down in a frown as he looked her over. It was obvious from his expression that he found her lacking but she refused to squirm. Gerry Brown was a nothing, no matter what he thought, and there was no doubt in her mind that she could do a better job than he could any day.

"You may as well go home and play with your dolls, sweet thing, because you're only wasting your time. We both know you don't have a shot. The job is already mine."

AJ clenched her fists behind her back. She would *not* let him get to her. "Really? Funny, I must have missed that inter-office memo. Not to mention your interview with the goalie."

"It's just a matter of time sweet thing. So why don't you go home and let the real men go to work?"

AJ was stopped from saying or doing anything she would

regret when the door opened behind her and a few of the players came out, talking noisily amongst themselves. Their conversation drifted off as they noticed the two of them standing there. AJ wondered what thoughts were going through their minds as they looked first at her then at Gerry.

The two obviously didn't fit in. AJ stood out in her jeans and sandals almost as much as Gerry stood out in his too-crisp slacks and stiff white shirt. She only hoped that nobody actually thought they were *together*. The thought made her groan out loud, which caught the attention of one of the players.

"Hey AJ. You okay?" It was Ian Donovan who asked the question. She nodded, surprised he remembered her. He had been a rookie the year that damned tabloid article came out with her name on it, and she hadn't really talked to him much.

"Yeah, I'm fine, thanks." She was getting ready to say something else, nothing in particular, just small talk to pass the time, when Gerry unceremoniously pushed her to the side with enough force that she stumbled. His phony smile widened and he thrust his hand in Ian's direction.

"Hi, Gerry Brown with The Times. I'm sure you've heard of me. That was a great game out there tonight, just great. I'd love to sit down and talk to you sometime. You know, put together a really great story."

AJ groaned again, almost embarrassed for Gerry. Did he not see how everyone was staring at him? His "great" approach was so superficial that a child could see through it. The few players that were standing around shifted uncomfortably as Ian sized him up and reluctantly shook his hand without saying anything. AJ noticed the looks being slid her way and she blurted out the first thing that came to her mind.

"We're not together!"

Several of the players were obviously amused at the desperation in her voice and she mentally kicked herself. This was not the best way to make good impressions.

Gerry turned to her with such a look of cold derision that she actually took a step back. From the look on his face, he had obviously decided she was bad for whatever impression he was trying to make. If he wanted to say something to her—and she was pretty sure he wanted to from the way his mouth was trying to form words—the sudden opening of the door stopped him. Literally. The metal slab slammed into him, forcing him to step back to avoid being flattened. AJ would have laughed except that she had to step back as well or risk having Gerry fall on top of her.

"What the—"

Voices erupted both in amusement and warning as the force behind the door stepped out into the chaos. AJ felt strong hands on her arms, pulling her out of harm's way as Gerry rounded on her with a scowl.

"You stupid little...don't you realize you're in my way? Why don't you just go home where you belong?"

AJ stared at him, stunned. She always knew there was something wrong with Gerry but she never would have credited him with such cold hatred and violence. And there was no doubt that the urge to do violence was there; she could see it in the coldness of his eyes and in the clenching of his fists as he stared her down. For a brief second she thought he might actually take a swing at her—if not for the solid body that suddenly stepped between them.

Alec's deep brown eyes drifted over her in what could have passed for concern before he turned to face Gerry, effectively shielding her with his size. Was it her imagination, or did his eyes get a few degrees chillier before he turned toward the moron?

"Is there something I can help you with?" Even Alec's voice seemed chillier than she recalled, not that Gerry noticed. Once again he thrust his hand forward for a handshake.

"Gerry Brown, The Times. We met the other day. Great game out there tonight, Alec. Really great. I was wondering if you wouldn't mind joining me for a cup of coffee so we could talk. It would make a great story."

AJ rolled her eyes, not caring that Gerry could see her. Was he always so transparent? It was a wonder he ever got interviews if this was his style.

"I'm not interested."

"But it would make for a great story—"

"I don't do interviews."

"Not at all, I understand. This isn't an interview, didn't mean to imply—"

"I'm not interested."

"Oh, I see. Not a problem. Maybe there's a chance—"

Almost casually, several of Alec's teammates worked their way in front of Gerry, effectively putting distance between the two. AJ was impressed at how smoothly they accomplished it, almost as if everything had been choreographed and rehearsed. Then again, knowing how adverse Alec was to the press, maybe this type of move *had* been rehearsed before.

And yet Gerry still didn't seem to get it, because he kept talking, leaning around a few of the players and trying to get closer to Alec. AJ rolled her eyes again and could have sworn she heard Alec chuckle. It was then that she realized his hand was still wrapped loosely around her elbow and that he was now leading her away from the small crowd.

So maybe Gerry wasn't the only one who was a little unobservant.

And while the sensation of the warm, callused hand against her skin wasn't unpleasant, it was beginning to become a little disconcerting now that she was aware of it. Little tingles radiated up her bare arm, causing her flesh to break out in tiny goose bumps.

"You wouldn't get so cold if you actually wore some clothes, you know. Where's the jacket you had on earlier?" Alec's voice was a bit harsher than she expected, considering his hand was still gently cupping her elbow as they walked into the parking garage. She cast a sideways look at him, surprised at the little flutter in her chest.

"Why the sudden obsession with my clothes? You make no sense Kolchak, none at all. Do you know that?"

"I am not obsessed with your clothes. I just don't think it's healthy to be in damp chilly air dressed like that."

AJ tried to smother her grunt of amusement but not very successfully. The noise only drew an irritated scowl from Alec, and he stopped and frowned at her. He seemed to realize he still had her elbow in his grasp because he suddenly let go and stepped back, looking awkward. The laughter AJ felt at his astonishment died in her throat. Alec's eyes grew darker as he studied her, and she couldn't quite seem to keep her stare from his mouth. She never noticed how full and soft his lips looked, and she wondered...

They both stepped back from each other at the same time, and AJ wondered if her foolish thoughts were written on her face. God, had she really just thought about how it would feel to be kissed by Alec Kolchak? She was losing her mind.

Alec cleared his throat and glanced around at the parked cars scattered around them. AJ briefly wondered what he was thinking then decided she was better off not knowing, especially if he had read her crazy thoughts on her face.

"So...where are you parked?"

"Huh? Oh, um, that's mine over there." AJ pointed toward her car, thinking the echo of the nearly-empty garage was playing tricks on her ears, because she thought his voice sounded a little huskier than normal. His head was turned away from her and the overhead lights threw shadows across his chiseled cheekbones and chin.

AJ swallowed, nervous for reasons she didn't want to explore, then walked toward her car. She could tell Alec was behind her from the sound of his footsteps, and she was only mildly surprised when he leaned in front of her to open the car door for her.

"So what exactly is going on, AJ?" Alec's eyes were dark and deep-set in the shadows, penetrating as he studied her. She shook her head and squeezed by him, lowering herself into the driver seat. Alec rested his arm along the doorframe, preventing her from closing the door. "C'mon AJ, out with it. What's going on? First I have you bugging me, and now that goofball. And please don't tell me he's a friend of yours."

"Uh, no, he's definitely not a friend, just some guy who works at the paper."

"The paper, hm?" Alec continued to study her, so intensely that she looked away and jammed the key into the ignition. The sound of the engine turning over erupted between them but wasn't loud enough to drown out his words.

"I'm not sure what game you're playing, AJ, but you can forget it now. I don't do interviews, so you can just pass that on to whoever needs to know. And I don't need people bothering me all season for something that's not going to happen."

"Alec—"

"Forget it, AJ. I don't need any headaches this season. And that goes for anyone else you might be working with. No interviews, period."

AJ studied Alec's face as he leaned closer to her. His expression was serious, his eyes warning her not to push. But she sensed something else beneath the dark look in his eyes and the warning scowl on his face. For just a second, there was something lurking behind the mask he presented her. But only for a second. AJ looked closer but whatever it had been was gone.

"I mean it, AJ. You've got a better chance of going one-on-one with me and scoring than you do of getting an interview. So just forget it. Okay?"

Alec gave her one last look, slammed her door shut, then turned and walked away. AJ watched his retreating form, not really seeing him as her mind latched onto an idea. Yeah, it was crazy. But that didn't mean it wouldn't work.

#

"You are absolutely insane."

AJ stared at Tim with as much anger as she dared while suppressing the urge to slug him. "I'm not insane. You have to at least let me try."

"Forget it, AJ. This has been going on for a week and neither one of you has gotten anywhere. I told you, I'm pulling the assignment. Which means Gerry will be the new columnist."

A cold chill swept through AJ at her editor's words. No! She had a chance, she knew it. If she could pull this off...

"That so totally sucks, Tim. And it's not impossible! At least give me the chance to try this one thing." Her words were rushed and desperate but she didn't care. She had to try. To just let this chance go without fighting...

"AJ, this wasn't some human interest story. You knew beforehand this wasn't going to be easy."

"Gerry didn't even get as far as I did. That has to count for something."

"But Gerry is used to more than human-interest pieces."

"Yeah? Did you know that jerk told me to go home and play with my dolls? *After* he called me 'sweet thing'? And it looked like he was ready to hit me, too. I can only imagine how that would look if I pursued it." AJ repressed her smile at Tim's wince, knowing what he was afraid of if she decided to push it. She wasn't afraid of a little blackmail. A quick minute passed by, just long enough to let the unspoken threat sink home. "Please, Tim. I'm capable of one hell of a lot more and you know it."

Tim watched her in complete silence, his face carefully blank as he rocked back and forth in his beat up chair. The rusty squeak-squeak grated on her nerves but she refused to let it bother her. "Resorting to blackmail and threats, hm?"

"I'm desperate."

Another long minute went by before he stopped the annoying rocking of the chair and tossed his pencil on the desk. "Fine. You have seventy-two hours. But this is the last chance. For *both* of you. And don't say a word!" Tim wagged a finger in her direction and she snapped her mouth closed. "Last shot, AJ. Seventy-two hours. After that, it's over."

Three days. AJ nodded, her mind reeling as she left Tim's office. Her hare-brained, crazy idea had every potential of blowing up in her face, but she was desperate.

And if this didn't work...well, at least she hadn't just rolled over and played dead while Gerry Brown danced over her corpse on his way to the new position.

THREE

Alec's focus was split, which was the last thing he needed. Pucks flew across the ice around him, hurtling toward him at unbelievable speeds, trying to get past him and gain entry into the net. He had been lucky so far, keeping his attention on the ice on front of him—which is where it needed to be.

But every once in a while his focus drifted, shifting off to the stands on his right. A metallic clank rang to his left and Alec grunted in frustration as he saw a puck shoot by his left foot. He lowered his stick to the ice and propped his elbow against the back of the net, muttering to himself. The goalie coach hollered something behind him, but Alec couldn't make it out. Not that he wanted to. The only positive thing so far was the fact that this wasn't a game.

Ian skated over to him, shaking his head with a look of amusement. "That one a rookie would have had, Kolchak." Ian tapped him with the blade of his stick then skated off. The barb was good-natured, but true.

Which frustrated Alec even more. There was no logical explanation for his distraction, no good reason why he was allowing such a minor nuisance to distract him this much. He shook his head and took another long drink of water then lowered himself into a crouch, waiting for the next onslaught of pucks. Focus, keep your eyes open, watch...

Alec mentally replayed the words over and over until they were nothing more than a distant hum in the back of his mind. Puck after puck was hurtled in his direction, and he deflected most of them, missing only the hardest and fastest shots.

A movement from the corner of his eye caught his attention and he glanced over. Just like that his concentration shattered. A second later he felt a dull thud as a puck connected solidly with the inside of his left foot. Alec grimaced and tightened his hold on his stick as he leaned forward, cursing.

The whistle blew but Alec barely heard it, still cursing to himself. Not because of his foot—the ache was minor and already fading. No, what had him cursing was the distraction in the stands.

Alec looked up again and frowned. It was bad enough that AJ was here, silently annoying him with her presence when he needed to focus on his game. But did she really need to be talking to Nathan Conners as well?

That was what had distracted him: looking up and seeing her talking to the team's offensive coach, saying something that actually had him laugh. Of all the people AJ should have the sense to leave alone, Nathan Conners was surely at the top of the list—especially after that article she wrote before he was forced into retirement with a knee injury. Alec couldn't even begin to understand why Nathan would talk with her.

The whistle blew again, signaling the end of practice. Alec shook his head, pushing all thoughts of AJ from his mind, and slowly skated toward the door. A long, hot shower then he would be heading home. He wanted nothing more than that—and to be left alone.

"Hey Alec."

The voice was friendly enough, maybe even a little hesitant, as if the speaker sensed his mood. Not great to begin with, it suddenly dropped a few notches. Alec sighed, loudly and with so much impatience that it had to be obvious to even the most casual observer, then turned around.

Not surprisingly, AJ was standing a few feet away from him, looking up at him with a combination of caution and stubbornness. He almost turned and walked away, but something stopped him. Maybe he was just too tired to be that rude.

"AJ, why do you keep bothering me?"

"Because I'm really into rejection."

He almost smiled at her sassy reply, at the way her chin tilted up a notch as she said it. Almost. He was too tired to be that amused, and afraid that any positive reaction would only encourage her more. Instead he rolled his eyes and shook his head. "Forget it AJ. The answer is no. You might as well just accept it and move on. It's not going to happen."

"What about a deal?"

"No deals."

"A bet, then?"

Alec chuckled to himself. AJ sounded almost desperate. He shook his head. "No bets."

"Alright then, how about a dare?"

That one almost got him. Or maybe it was the sly look in AJ's eyes. A dare? Did she really think he would agree to a childish dare? He was half-tempted to say yes, just to see what reaction he'd get. In fact, he actually opened his mouth to speak but was interrupted by an even more annoying presence that appeared from nowhere.

"Kolchak, Gerry Brown, we met the other night. Great practice out there."

Alec turned to face the intruder as one thought came to mind.

"What a moron."

Alec froze, wondering if he had said it out loud, then realized the phrase had been muttered by AJ. Gerry Brown either didn't hear her, or chose to ignore her, because he continued to stare up at Alec with a gleam in his eyes.

"No. No interviews. I thought this was a closed practice anyway." Alec looked around, his humor taking a turn for the worse, and felt a brief sense of relief when he saw Nathan walking toward them. "Nathan, wasn't this a closed practice?"

Nathan shrugged, obviously not aware of what was going on. Alec turned back, his expression as cool as he could make it without actually scowling. "No interviews. I was just telling your associate here—"

"Oh, rest assured Alec that we're not associates." Gerry straightened to his fully inadequate height and nodded, a flat smile on his pale face. "I'm a professional, not some wannabe bimbo who isn't smart enough to know her own place."

The callous words echoed then died away in the absolute silence that suddenly surrounded them. Alec couldn't believe his own ears, and if it hadn't been for the reactions around him, he would have sworn he had imagined the words.

A couple of the players gathered nearby edged closer, their postures erect and stiff. Even Nathan looked defensive. But the reaction that stood out the most was AJ's.

It was the exact opposite of what Alec would expect from her. Instead of standing tall and looking eager to take the guy on, her entire posture was defeated. Her shoulders slumped and her head hung low, as if she had been beaten terribly in some major game. Alec couldn't see much of her face because it was covered by her hair, but what he could see was red and blotchy. Quickly he looked away, not wanting to see if there were tears in her eyes, not caring for the protective feeling that rippled through him at the thought.

But Gerry Brown stood there as if nothing had happened, as if his words had gone unnoticed. Or worse, as if they were acceptable and he expected everyone to agree with him. Anger swept through Alec, cold and quick, and he opened his mouth to speak. Nathan's hand clamped down on his shoulder with enough force to stop him.

"Actually Alec, Mr. Brown's viewpoint aside, I think any sports writer should at least have some knowledge and enjoyment of the game, don't you?"

Alec stared at Nathan as if he had lost his mind. Maybe he had, because his words had absolutely nothing to do with the current situation.

"You see, AJ and I were talking, and she had a little proposition for you."

"I don't think—"

Gerry Brown interrupted AJ with a snort of laughter. "A *proposition*. Of course she did."

"Actually Mr. Brown, it was a very interesting proposal. Maybe you'd be willing to do the same."

AJ was now squirming and shaking her head, visibly uncomfortable at whatever Nathan was about to say. The fact that she seemed suddenly unable to talk peaked Alec's interest, because he had never seen her speechless. He motioned for Nathan to continue. "What kind of proposal?"

"A little one-on-one. Or maybe one-or-two, if Mr. Brown is interested."

Alec raised his brow, confused. He wasn't quite sure where Nathan was leading him, and he didn't know if he wanted to find out.

"One-on-one?"

"Not one-on-one." AJ finally spoke up, her voice still more subdued than Alec was used to. She faced him again, some of her stubbornness coming back as he watched. "A shoot-out."

"What?" It wasn't what Alec expected to hear. "You want a shoot-out?"

"Well, yeah. Kinda."

"You're kidding."

"No, I'm not kidding. I get five chances. If I can score just once, you agree to let me do a story on you."

"You're kidding." Alec couldn't stop his chuckle, not sure which was funnier: that she thought he'd agree, or that she thought she had a chance. "No way."

"Why not?"

"Because it's ridiculous, that's why."

"Why? Are you afraid I might actually get one across the line?"

AJ stared at him, her hands fisted on her hips, the stubborn gleam back in her eye. Alec felt his eyes drawn to the shirt pulled tight across her chest and he had an irrational urge to shake some sense into her. The urge had nothing to do with what she was proposing, which irritated him even more.

Several of the players watched him, waiting for his answer. Alec glanced around at them then at Nathan, and saw the corner of his mouth twitch in a smile he was obviously trying not to show. He tried to think of a way to say no without looking stupid. He had nothing to worry about—there was no way AJ would be able to get a puck by him.

So what reason could he possibly have to say no?

Alec clenched his jaw and swore to himself.

"Okay, you're on. And I'll do one even better. Five chances to cross the line. Do it just once, and I'm yours for a month, twenty-four/seven. How's that sound?" He readjusted his grip on the goalie stick and lowered his helmet. "Nathan, get them suited up. I don't want them getting hurt."

"What?" AJ's voice was a squeak of disbelief. "You want to do this now?"

He faced her before she could speak again. "Now or never sweetheart. What's it going to be?"

"Uh..." AJ studied him for a few seconds then nodded, her lips pursed in an obvious attempt to stop herself from saying anything else. He smiled at her then faced Gerry Brown.

"And you Mr. Brown...now or never. What's it going to be?"

"I would certainly never—"

"Good, just what I wanted to hear. Somebody get him out of here. And Mr. Brown, I never want to see you again. Is that clear?" Alec didn't even wait to see what the reporter would do, just turned and walked back to the ice.

This whole thing was ridiculous. There was no way AJ would score. But if he had to play this little game to be left in peace, then he would. At least he had managed to get one of them out of his hair. With any luck, the other one would be gone in a matter of minutes as well.

Alec ignored the weird feeling that last thought gave him as his blades hit the ice.

#

"Oh my God, what have I done?" AJ muttered the phrase under her breath for the hundredth time. She wanted to rub her chest but she couldn't reach it under the thick pads now covering her. She wanted to go home and curl up in a dark corner and forget about the whole thing.

Me and my bright ideas.

"Are you going to be okay?"

AJ snapped her head up and looked at Ian. The poor guy had been given the job of helping her get dressed in the pads, and she almost felt sorry for him. Almost. Between her nervousness and the threat of an impending migraine, she was too preoccupied to muster much sympathy for anyone else right now.

"Yeah, I'm fine." She took a deep breath and stood, wobbling for only a second on the skates. This was not how she had imagined the bet going. When she cooked up the stupid idea, she had figured on having a few days to at least practice.

Well, not really. If she was honest with herself, she never even imagined that Alec would agree to it. But if he had, then she would have had a few days to practice.

So much for her imagination.

She took another deep breath then followed Ian from the locker room. It didn't take too long for her gait to even out and she muttered a thankful prayer. She only hoped that she didn't sprawl face-first as soon as she stepped on the ice.

Her right hand clenched around the stick, getting used to the feel of it, getting used to the fit of the bulky glove—which was too big to begin with. This would have been so much easier if all she had to do was put on a pair of skates. She had never considered the possibility of having to put all the gear on, right down to the helmet that was a heavy weight bearing down on her head.

She really needed to do something with her imagination and its lack of thinking things all the way through.

AJ took another deep breath when they finally reached the ice. She reached out to open the door but was stopped by Ian.

"Listen, AJ, I'm not even going to pretend I know what's going on or why you think you can do this, but I'll give you some advice. Shoot fast and low, and aim for the five and two holes—those are Alec's weak spots. The five hole is—"

"Between the legs, I know." AJ winced at the sharpness of her voice. Ian was only trying to help her. He had no reason to realize she knew anything about ice hockey, and not just because she liked to write about it. She offered him a smile to take the bite from her words then slammed the butt of the stick down against the door latch so it would swing open. Two steps later and she was standing on a solid sheet of thick ice.

AJ breathed deeply several times then slowly made her way to the other side of the rink, where Alec was nonchalantly leaning against the top post of the net talking to Nathan. They both watched as she skated up to them and came to a smooth stop. Alec's face was expressionless as he studied her, and she wondered what thoughts were going through his mind. Probably nothing she really wanted to know.

Nathan nodded at her, offering a small smile. She had to give the guy some credit for not laughing in her face when she asked his opinion on her idea. "Well, at least it looks like you've been on skates before. That's a plus."

AJ didn't say anything, just absently nodded in his direction. The carefree attitude she had been aiming for was destroyed by the helmet sliding down over her forehead. She pushed it back on her head then glanced at the five pucks lined neatly on the goal line. All she had to do was get one of them across. Just one.

She didn't have a chance.

She pushed the pessimistic thought to the back of her mind. "So, do I get a chance to warm up or take a practice shot?"

Alec sized her up then briskly shook his head. "No."

AJ swallowed and glanced at the pucks, then back at Alec. "Alrighty then. A man of few words. That's what I like about you, Kolchak." AJ though he might have cracked a smile behind his mask but she couldn't be sure. She sighed and leaned on her stick, trying to look casual and hoping it didn't slip out from under her and send her sprawling. "So, what are the rules?"

"Simple. You get five chances to shoot. If you score, you win. If you don't, I win." Alec swept the pucks to the side with the blade of his stick so Nathan could pick them up. She followed the moves with her eyes and tried to ignore the pounding in her chest.

She had so much riding on this. Something told her that Alec was dead serious about being left alone if she lost. It had been a stupid idea, and she wondered if she would have had better luck at trying to wear him down the old-fashioned way.

She studied his posture and decided probably not. He had been mostly patient with her up to this point, but even she knew he would have reached his limit soon.

"All or nothing, then. Fair enough. So, are you ready?"

AJ didn't hear his response but thought it was probably something sarcastic. She sighed then turned to follow Nathan to the center line, her heart beating too fast as her feet glided across the ice. She shrugged her shoulders, trying to readjust the bulk of the pads, and watched as Nathan lined the pucks up.

He finished then straightened and faced her, an unreadable expression on his face. He finally grinned and shook his head.

"I have no idea if you know what you're doing or not, but good luck. You're going to need it."

"Gee, thanks."

Nathan walked across the ice to the bench and leaned against the outer boards, joining a few of the other players gathered there. AJ wished they were gone, that they had something better to do than stand around and watch her make a fool of herself.

Well, she had brought it on herself.

She closed her eyes and inhaled deeply, pushing everything from her mind except what she was about to do. When she opened her eyes again, her gaze was on the first puck. Heavy, solid...nothing more than a slab of black rubber...

Okay, so she wasn't going to have any luck becoming one with the puck. Stupid idea. AJ had never understood that whole Zen thing anyway.

She swallowed and began skating in small circles, testing her ankles as she turned first one way then another, testing the stick as she swept it back and forth across the ice in front of her. Not too bad. Maybe she hadn't forgotten—

"Sometime today would be nice!"

AJ winced at the sarcasm in Alec's voice, and wished she had some kind of comeback for him. Instead she mumbled to herself and got into position behind the first puck. She didn't even look up to see if he was ready. Didn't ask if it was okay to start, she just pushed off hard and skated, the stick out in front of her.

This was her one shot, she couldn't blow it.

FOUR

AJ surprised herself with how quickly she gathered speed. The net loomed ahead of her, getting closer as she skated. Her mind focused on the net, on the puck cradled against her stick as she moved forward...

And on Alec standing oh-so-casually between the pipes, acting as if she was no threat at all. The jerk.

She took a deep breath and crouched lower, then pulled back on the stick and shot forward with it in one quick move to send the puck flying...

Too wide, it hit the outside of the net and harmlessly bounced off, sliding to the edge of the boards.

"That was one." Alec's voice sounded bored, but AJ was gratified to see that at least he was paying a little more attention. She had pulled back and shot too soon, irritated at his stance. Maybe she didn't really have a chance, but she wasn't completely hopeless, either.

AJ returned to center ice and puck number two, shooting a little better this time and actually hitting the post. The third time was even more gratifying because Alec had to reach out and stop the puck, neatly pulling it into his glove and cradling it against his chest. She skated around the back of the net and could have sworn she glimpsed an expression of surprise on his face as she went by him.

AJ had to aim lower, go for the five hole like Ian had suggested. But she wasn't sure she could control her shot that well. Her last three passes had succeeded in bringing her comfort level back up, but it had literally been years since she played hockey with her brother.

Never that great to begin with, she was pretty sure she didn't have the skill necessary now. Her legs had turned into rubber, her breath was coming in short gasps, and her body was covered in sweat. A dull throb was building at the base of her skull, and she was very much afraid that it wasn't from the helmet. Now would be the worst time for one of her migraines to strike.

Two more shots, that was all she had. All or nothing, AJ knew it came down to this.

Just two more shots.

She closed her eyes and took a deep breath, then skated up to the fourth puck and took off. No more straight shots, they were too easy for Alec. Instead she skated back and forth, cutting side to side, hoping she could at least catch him off guard enough to...

One last deep breath and she lunged forward with her stick, hitting the puck with all the strength she could muster to send it flying. She lost her balance at the last minute and fell with a jaw-snapping thud, sliding toward the net on her back at break-neck speed.

For as fast as she was going, everything else moved in slow motion. AJ's eyes followed the puck as it flew through the air, straight toward the back of the net. Alec's catching hand reached out for it, barely tipping the edge of the puck as it sped past him, his eyes focused more on her. She kept sliding toward him, unable to stop and not really caring as the puck hit the back of the net with a soft whoosh.

AJ would have jumped for joy if she hadn't still been sliding. The puck made it past Alec! She won!

Her enjoyment only lasted a brief second before she careened into Alec's legs, sending him tumbling across her lower body as they both crashed into the net. A flash of pain throbbed through AJ's back and shoulder as she slammed against the outside post but she ignored it.

"Yes! Yes!" Her voice was muffled but she didn't care—she wasn't yelling for anyone else but herself.

"Holy shit, are you okay? AJ? Are you hurt?" Alec clambered from on top of her, sliding toward her head on his knees. His helmet and gloves were gone and his brown eyes were wide with concern. AJ waved off his worry, still flat on her back, and lifted her stick in a little victory shake.

"I did it! I actually did it!"

"Never mind that, are you hurt?"

More voices surrounded her, the words jumbled so she could only make out a few here and there. AJ started to push herself up then winced slightly at the pain in her left arm and fell back to the ice. Instantly Alec was beside her again, his strong arms coming around her as he helped her stand, then steadying her as she wobbled slightly on the skates.

Her breath caught in her throat at the look in his eyes and she quickly stepped backward, almost sending them both back down to the ice. His hold tightened around her and for that quick moment, it was just the two of them on the ice by themselves.

AJ swallowed then allowed herself a quick smile, not knowing exactly what the look on Alec's face meant. There was a very real possibility that he wouldn't be pleased with the fact that she had actually managed to score. And she knew he couldn't be pleased with the prospect of having to give her an interview.

Alec's hand reached toward her, and she braced herself for some scathing or sarcastic remark. Instead, he just continued looking at her with those dark eyes as he gently removed the helmet from her head. AJ ignored the throbbing at the base of her skull and held her breath as Alec brushed her sweat-soaked hair off her forehead. The air around her grew suddenly warmer and she was almost afraid to move, let alone say anything. But the silence worried her, and she decided it would be better to just get everything over with now while she could still stand.

"So does this mean I won?"

A few long seconds went by before Alec finally gave her a brief smile.

"Yeah, you won."

"Cool, because I think I'm going to collapse now."

#

AJ pulled the towel off her head and shook out her wet hair, only half-heartedly finger-combing it before turning her attention to the bruise that spread up the back of her arm to her shoulder. An ugly combination of dark blue and purple, it ran along the back and side of her arm from her shoulder to just above her elbow. It was almost the exact shape of the goal post and hurt like hell.

AJ couldn't stop the smile that crept across her face. She still couldn't quite believe it. She had actually scored against Alec Kolchak! She was going to interview him and get her story!

Her mind was already planning the course of her interview with Alec. Who was she kidding? She had been planning this since Tim had put the challenge out there! It was going to be extensive and in-depth, giving him the attention and recognition he deserved as a goalie.

And giving her the chance at the staff spot at the paper.

Her thoughts of making Gerry Brown crawl back under his rock as she put him in his place were interrupted by the doorbell. AJ winced as the echo bounced around the inside of her skull, and she made a mental note to finally go and get her migraine prescription refilled after she got rid of whoever was at the door.

She threw on a pair of loose gym shorts and a sports bra then walked the short distance from her bathroom to the front door. She wasn't expecting company and wasn't in the mood for any, not when all she wanted to do was lie down and relive her victory from a few hours ago. Her mouth dropped open in surprise when she opened the door and saw Alec standing there. She smothered a laugh when he quickly turned his back to her.

"Shit AJ. Do you always open the door half-naked?"

"Uh..." AJ snapped her mouth closed and glanced down at herself, wondering if maybe she forgot something important, like her shorts. No, she was completely dressed. "I have clothes on."

"You're missing your shirt."

"Oh, get over it Kolchak. It's a sports bra. I'm in my own apartment!"

Alec glanced at her over his shoulder, and AJ was surprised to see a faint blush tinge his cheeks. It amazed her. What on earth did Alec Kolchak have to blush about?

"Yeah, well...you shouldn't walk around half-naked."

"Uh..." Hearing the word *naked* coming from Alec's mouth suddenly made the room seem smaller and hotter and for once in her life AJ couldn't think of anything to say. Which was probably a good thing.

"Actually, for this it's probably better. Come here." Alec grabbed her hand as he walked by her into her living room, tugging her along. AJ swore her heart stopped beating. She held her breath in anticipation then let it out silently when he none-too-gently led her to the sofa and pushed her down. "Sit and let me look at your shoulder."

"What?"

"I said, let me look at your shoulder," he repeated. AJ was stunned into silence as he gently pushed around the bruise, twisting and turning so that she was directly facing him as he bent over her. She swallowed as her eyes rested at his waist-level. Well, not exactly his waist, a little lower...

AJ swallowed again. The jeans he was wearing were old and worn, snug in just the right spots so that her imagination caught fire...

"Ouch! Hey, that hurt!" AJ twisted away from him, the burning pain in her shoulder putting an effective stop to her completely uncharacteristic thoughts. She placed her hand up to protect herself from anymore of his prodding, and hissed in surprise when his own hand covered hers in a gentle touch.

"I'm sorry. I didn't mean to make it worse. Here, let me see it again." Alec laced his fingers through hers and moved her hand away. Instead of releasing it, though, he kept it loosely held in his as he continued to examine the bruise. AJ sucked her breath in again, but it had nothing to do with the pain her shoulder.

In fact, she could barely feel the pain. All she could feel was the warm caress of his touch as he gently massaged the bruise, the strength of his fingers laced with hers as he continued to hold her hand. AJ turned her head away in case he could see her face, then immediately closed her eyes. He was standing so close to her, his hips only inches away from her face. All she had to do was...

AJ bit back a moan and willed her breathing to return to normal. There was no way Alec should be affecting her like this. No way. Yeah, he was attractive...well, no, actually, he was gorgeous, but...No, she was *not* attracted to him. She couldn't be.

"You can open your eyes now, I'm done."

"Huh?"

"I said, I'm done. I'm not going to poke you anymore."

"Oh. Uh, okay." AJ bit back another moan as he released her hand and stepped away. At least she could breathe normally now.

Sort of. "So...what are you doing here, anyway?"

"I came to pick you up. Are you packed?"

"What?"

"I said, are you packed? Are you sure you didn't hit your head this morning?"

"No I didn't hit my head!" AJ stood up, hoping for any small advantage to help her out. For some reason, she was having trouble understanding anything Alec was saying. The feeling was disconcerting and left her more than a little rattled. "Why would I be packed?"

"Your interview. You won the bet, right?"

"Well, yeah, but...what do I have to pack for?" AJ knew she sounded dim-witted and she hated that, hated playing into the perception too many people had about her based on her appearance, but she honestly had no idea what Alec was talking about.

"The bet was that if you won, you had me for a month, twenty-four/seven. So unless you plan on wearing...that," he motioned at her from head-to-toe, the expression on his face almost comical, "for the next month, you should go pack."

"But pack for what? Where is it I'm supposed to be going?"

Alec took a step toward her, an unreadable expression in his eyes. For a quick second, looking down at her like that, he seemed so much taller, so much bigger. But it was just an illusion, gone when AJ blinked. He had turned away already and was strolling down the short hallway to her bedroom.

"You're going home with me. How else did you expect this to work?"

AJ's mouth dropped open at his words, but thankfully he couldn't see how off-guard he caught her—he was already in her bedroom, out of her sight. She stood frozen for a few seconds then raced down the hallway after him, his words not making any sense.

"But...hey! What are you doing?" AJ closed the distance to her dresser and pulled the clothing from his hand, inwardly wincing when she realized he was going through her underwear drawer. She stuffed the lace undergarments back in the drawer and slammed it shut, trying hard to keep her mind focused on something *other* than Alec Kolchak's large hands caressing her lingerie. Not that he had been caressing them, but still...

"I am not going home with you. Don't be ridiculous."

"Then how were you going to accomplish this thing?"

"Thing? Thing? It's an interview, Kolchak, not a 'thing'. And I was going to do it like every other interview: by asking you questions. That's how these 'things' usually work."

Alec raised one brow at her then slowly smiled and nodded. Before she realized it, he was sitting on the edge of her bed, his hands loosely clasped between his spread legs as he stared up at her. The sight of him on her bed, of his lopsided grin and the day-old stubble on his jaw, sent more crazy thoughts through her mind, which made her wince. What was with her lately? This was Alec Kolchak, her annoying roadblock to her fantasy job. Since when did she look at him as anything else?

"So then ask."

"Huh?"

"I said, then ask. You're the reporter. Interview me."

"I can't interview you right now!"

"Why not? That's what you do, isn't it?"

"Yes, but—"

"Then do it."

"I..." AJ's voice faded and she clamped her lips so tightly together they almost hurt. She mentally counted to five then let out a deep and exasperated breath. "I cannot interview you while you're sitting on my bed. It's not done that way. I have a whole list of things—"

"Okay, fine. Here's the deal." Alec stood and closed the distance between them, so close that AJ could smell the faint scent of soap on his skin, could feel the warmth radiating from his body. "We either do the interview right here and now, or you pack some things, come home with me and do it by the terms of the bet."

Alec stared at her, his eyes almost daring as he held a large duffle bag between them. Funny, but AJ hadn't noticed it earlier, and she wondered briefly how he had gotten it out of her closet without her realizing it.

"You have one minute to decide."

AJ looked up at Alec, into his dark eyes, and felt a funny flip in her stomach. She had no idea what he was up to and she had a feeling that this whole plan of hers was about to backfire. But in the end, she really didn't have much choice.

She clenched her jaw and yanked the duffel bag from Alec's hand. "Fine. I'll meet you in the living room in five minutes."

#

Alec sat on the sofa, staring at the wide-screen TV in front of him without really seeing it. His attention was focused more on the girl curled up on the recliner, her legs tucked under her, a frown on her face, papers scattered across her lap.

She had been sitting that way for at least two hours and Alec wondered why her legs hadn't fallen asleep yet. Except for reaching up and rubbing her temples with a wince every few minutes, she hadn't really moved. If he sat that way for any length of time, not moving, he'd not only have leg cramps, he'd start to go insane with the inactivity.

His hand clenched momentarily around the soda can he was holding and he resisted the urge to stretch his own legs. AJ paused in jotting down whatever she had been writing and looked over at him, her face almost serene in its blankness. A few seconds went by before her blue eyes cleared and one corner of her mouth tilted ever-so-slightly, as if she just realized where she was. It occurred to Alec that she had been so lost in whatever she had been doing that she really had been somewhere else, at least mentally.

The thought almost scared Alec. Not just because it was evidently very easy for her to lose herself like that. No, what worried him was that he was fairly certain that he had figured at least a little bit in wherever she had been mentally. And he did not like the idea of someone being so focused on him...unless, of course, that someone was in bed with him. Then being focused on... He shook his head, wondering where in the hell that idea had come from.

"Are you okay?"

Her question, asked so quietly in the stillness of the living room, caught him off-guard. Alec took the last sip of the soda, trying not to look at her too much. "I was just wondering the same about you. How can you sit so still like that for so long? That would drive me crazy."

AJ stretched her legs out in front of her, making a small little noise of contentment as she did so. Alec swallowed and tried not to notice the shapely length of her calves, or the way her bare toes wiggled as if she was trying to restore circulation to them. He suddenly wished that he hadn't offered to keep her company earlier, that he had just disappeared into another part of the spacious condo once they had gotten here.

But the thought of her wandering around, nosing through his personal things, had stopped him from making his own exit. Oddly enough, though, she hadn't seemed very interested in looking around. Other than the brief tour when he had carried her bags to the spare room, she had pretty much stayed curled up on the recliner. In fact, except for pausing on the downstairs balcony and openly admiring the waterfront view of the harbor, she didn't appear to be interested in anything other than the papers in her lap.

"It doesn't bother me. I guess I'm just used to it."

It took a second before Alec understood what she was talking about, that she was only answering his question from not even a minute ago. He raised the soda can to his lips before realizing it was already empty, then hastily sat it down on the coffee table in front of him. He searched for something to say, but nothing came to mind readily, so he reverted back to a question he knew he had already asked her.

"So, what is that stuff you're so engrossed in, anyway?"

AJ reshuffled the papers in her lap then arranged them into a neat pile before placing them on the side table next to her. She reached around and turned off the reading light behind the recliner, suddenly casting herself in shadows. She winced, then quickly rubbed her temples before facing him. Her blue eyes were suddenly darker as she turned her gaze on him.

"I told you, just background stuff I might use for filler. Not that there's much background info out there on you. At least, not much more than what I already knew."

"You do know that it's really weird to hear you talk about me like that, right? Like I'm some kind of...of...I don't know what. Like an object or something."

"Trust me, Alec, you're not an object. All that's in here," she looked away long enough to tap the pile of papers to her left, "is a bunch of dry, boring statistics. You know: when you were drafted, games played, average saves, blah, blah, blah. Absolutely nothing personal or informative or even interesting. It's all superficial. I told you before that you were more than welcome to look it over if you wanted to."

"No, I'll pass."

She tilted her head to the side and quietly studied him, her expression thoughtful. "Suit yourself. But I'll be honest. For someone who's been in the public eye for as long as you have, it's remarkable that there's nothing more out there about you. It's like...I don't know, it's like you've deliberately hid behind this blank wall, and you've done it so well that people stay away from you."

"I happen to like my privacy. My life is my business, nobody else's." Alec hadn't meant for the words to come out so harsh, but she had hit too close to the truth.

"Alec, there's nothing wrong with privacy. I like mine, too. But there's a difference between being private, and hiding." She gestured again at the papers. "This stuff isn't just boring, it screams that you're hiding from life."

Again, her words hit too close to the truth. But phrased the way they were made him sound like a recluse, a hermit who wanted no involvement with the world around him. But that wasn't him. He just liked...being private. He stood up, planning on getting another drink, but stopped. He cleared his throat and then asked his own question to change the subject.

"So if it's all that boring, how you could get so wrapped up in it for the last few hours?"

AJ laughed, a soft sound in the surrounding quiet that had a surprising effect on Alec, one that he didn't even want to acknowledge. She lifted herself from the recliner and walked by him, passing so closely he imagined he could feel the heat radiating from her. Alec stepped back involuntarily, once again caught off-guard by his body's reaction to her. And once again, he blamed it on stress and lack of sleep.

AJ stopped less than a foot from him, staring up at him with those blue eyes that suddenly sparkled in the low light. A half-smile curved her lips and she folded her arms across her chest. Alec's eyes automatically drifted down, and he had to force himself not to stare at the fullness of her chest and the painfully appealing amount of cleavage revealed with her arms crossed like that.

"I wasn't 'wrapped up' in it, as you say. I was thinking about the best way to approach this whole interview, the best way to get you to open up without having you think I'm going to cut your heart out and use it to finger paint my article." She looked at him for a few more seconds, a flash of disappointment sparking in her eyes, then turned and headed for the stairway.

AJ paused, her bare foot resting on the bottom step, and looked back at him one more time. Alec swore her eyes were even darker now, a sense of something resembling disappointment reflected in their depths. "And Alec, could you do me a favor?" Her voice was quiet, barely more than a whisper and laced with some quiet emotion he couldn't name.

"What?"

"Could you please stop staring at my chest whenever I talk to you? You claim you're afraid of being treated as an object, that people see only what they want to see and that everything is superficial. But you're doing the exact same thing to me that you've accused everyone else of doing to you. I gave you credit for being better than that."

FIVE

Alec stood immobilized for long moments after AJ disappeared upstairs, not quite believing her last words. Had he really been that obvious?

He thought back over their last few encounters. Not only had he been obvious, there were times when he had been downright rude. Never once had it occurred to him that she would be bothered by his comments or his glances. She had never indicated that she even noticed, let alone was upset by it until tonight.

No, he realized, that wasn't exactly true. Now that he thought about it, there had been times when AJ had made remarks to him, subtle or even sarcastic. But not once did he ever stop to consider...

Calling himself a complete moron, he walked through the downstairs and turned off the lights, muttering to himself as he did so. His footsteps were heavy as he climbed the stairs, pausing briefly outside the closed door of the small guest room he had shown AJ hours earlier. Guilt went through him, quick and dull. It was the smallest of the three guest rooms in the sprawling condo. Definitely functional but nowhere near as roomy as the others. He could have at least given her one of the spare rooms that had its own bath so she could have some privacy.

Alec shook his head and continued down the hall to his own room, his thoughts still turning inward. Was he really as shallow and callous as that? Was he really that inconsiderate?

He ripped the shirt over his head and tossed it toward the clothes hamper on his way to the bathroom. Turning the faucet as cold as it would it go, he leaned over the sink and splashed water over his face, shivering slightly as it dripped onto his chest and ran down his stomach. Alec pulled a towel from the rack and rubbed it over his face and chest.

Tomorrow he would move her into one of the other rooms. The thought didn't do much to relieve the guilt he felt, though. For so many years he had felt the frustration of people judging him only for what they saw on the surface, or making certain assumptions based on what they saw instead of who he was. Beyond the frustration was anger that people could be so shallow, so superficial.

The realization that he was the same, that he had been guilty of doing just that, ate at him with a sour burning. Alec splashed more water over his face to wash away the feeling, refusing to look at his reflection in the mirror.

The dark thoughts stayed with him as he left the bathroom. He pulled back the covers on the large bed then turned off the light, pausing as his eyes adjusted to the darkness. The room wasn't completely black—lights from the harbor twinkled through the French doors leading to the private balcony, and he stared at their reflection in the glass.

AJ had accused him of hiding. He didn't agree with her. There was a difference between hiding and valuing privacy. Just because he didn't want people in his business didn't mean he was hiding. But lately, there had been this feeling of...something missing. Not emptiness, but not quite a completeness, either. Hell, he didn't know how to describe it, and he didn't think it was really worth looking into, either. It was just a phase, one he was sure would go away.

But he couldn't shake the uncomfortable feeling that AJ had gotten just a little too close with her observations.

Sighing with a weariness he understood but didn't want to acknowledge just yet, Alec moved to stand at the balcony doors. He tended to stare out at the lights reflected on the black surface of the harbor and just think. Or sometimes he just stared, his mind blank as a peaceful quiet seeped through him.

The peaceful quiet wasn't coming tonight, he already knew that. With another sigh he turned away from the balcony and walked out of the room and across the hall. He didn't need a psychic to tell him he was getting ready to make a mistake: *that* was going to be a given. But maybe he could ease just enough of the guilt to let him sleep.

Alec hesitated in front of AJ's room for a second, then rapped lightly on the door with his knuckles. Silence greeted him so he knocked again, a little harder this time. There was still no response. Surely she hadn't fallen asleep that quickly, had she? He envied her if she had. Very rarely would his mind succumb to the sleep his body asked for; too many thoughts whirled around him at night.

Alec knocked once more, deciding that if there was no answer, he would leave well enough alone and rectify his guilt in the morning. He was just about to walk away when he heard shuffling behind the closed door. A few seconds later, the door slowly opened. AJ stood on the other side, wearing nothing but an oversized t-shirt that barely came to the top of her thighs. Alec swallowed, hard, at the sight of her long bare legs, and was about to say something when he noticed the rest of her.

She looked like shit.

Her hair was disheveled, damp strands clinging to her cheeks as she held the side of the door in a white-knuckled grip. Her eyes squinted up at him, and he could see that they were rimmed in red. At first he thought she might have been crying, but as he looked closer he realized her face was pinched in what looked like pain.

His next thought was that her arm and shoulder must hurt more than he realized. Alec took a step closer to her then stopped when she didn't move to open the door more than the few inches she already had. He pushed on it gently, only a little surprised that she took a step back to allow it. Her eyes squinted shut and she looked away.

"AJ, what is it? Is it your shoulder?" He was closing the little bit of distance between them when she stepped back, nearly stumbling. She mumbled something that sounded like "lights" as she made her way back to the bed, gingerly groping for the edge before tumbling back onto it. She flung one arm over her eyes as her left leg dangled over the edge, almost as if she didn't have the energy to pull it the rest of the way onto the mattress.

Alec paused half-way into the room, not knowing what he should do. She looked awful, and even he could tell that something was wrong, something more than just the bumps and bruises she had earned earlier that afternoon.

The soft whimper coming from the bed caused him to move further into the room instead of leaving. There was something so needful, so vulnerable in the sound that he had to at least offer to help. But first he needed to find out what was wrong.

Alec approached the bed warily. The only light in the room was the weak light shining in from further down the hallway. It was barely enough for him to make out AJ's figure on the bed.

"AJ? What is it? What's wrong?" He reached out a tentative hand and placed it on the arm covering her eyes. He was surprised when she flinched, even more surprised at the cold clamminess of her skin.

"Don't." The quiet word was hardly a whisper but still commanding. Alec swiftly removed his hand from her arm then stood there, feeling helpless.

"Is it your shoulder? Do you need me—"

"Migraine. No noise."

"Oh." A migraine? She had that much pain from a headache? Alec shifted on his feet and glanced around the dark room, wondering what to do. Should he just leave her alone? Or should he try to do something? Was there even anything he could do?

Alec turned toward the door and reached out to close it. He had no idea what he could do to help her, but he couldn't just leave her alone, not when she was obviously in pain.

Another whimper came from the direction of the bed, a little sharper and more drawn out this time. From the sound, Alec guessed that she thought he must have left the room. He didn't think for a second that AJ would allow anyone to see any kind of weakness coming from her, especially him. Well, she would just have to deal with it.

He closed the distance to the bed then gently lifted her leg the rest of the way onto the mattress. Her body stiffened for a quick second at his touch, telling him again that she had thought he left. Alec felt a rush of disappointment at the realization but quickly squashed it; he hadn't exactly been warm to her the last couple of weeks so why would she expect anything different now?

"Tell me how to help, AJ."

Several long minutes went by. Alec was beginning to think she had either drifted off or was ignoring him before she finally spoke, her voice so quiet he had to lean so close to hear her that his forehead nearly touched her arm. Even then he couldn't make out everything she said.

But he heard enough to realize she was asking for a cold cloth. He hurried from the room, mindful of making too much noise, and quickly returned with a cold wet washcloth. He also had a bottle of prescription-strength ibuprofen and a glass of water.

Alec lowered himself on the bed next to AJ, doing his best not to jostle her. "I brought some aspirin. Would that help?"

She barely nodded her head then tried to push herself to a sitting position. The obvious pain that little bit of movement caused her made Alec wince, and he quickly put his arm behind her shoulders and propped her up just enough that she could wash the pills down.

Instead of letting her lay back down on the mattress, Alec shifted his position behind her so that her head was resting on his stomach. Belatedly he realized that it wasn't the most comfortable position for him: his back was against the headboard but he was slouching too much. There was no doubt his back would be screaming in stiffness before long. But it seemed to be comfortable for AJ so he didn't say anything, just sat there and laid the cold cloth over her eyes.

It wasn't long before Alec realized he was stroking the hair back from her face. He paused, surprised at the intimacy of his actions, then continued. It seemed to be relaxing her, and it certainly wasn't hurting him.

A little while later, Alec was forced to reevaluate his earlier assumption. He wasn't hurting, but he was quickly becoming uncomfortable.

AJ's hair was fanned across his stomach, the soft strands tickling the skin at the waistband of his gym shorts. The silky smoothness of her hair in his hands and on his skin was causing his body to react in a way that surprised him. Yeah, he had felt some currents between them. No, he wasn't stupid enough to deny the fact that she was attractive. But that didn't mean he was attracted *to* her. Which was why his body's reaction caught him by surprise.

But maybe it shouldn't be. AJ had a lush body, he couldn't deny that. And he was a guy. He doubted that there were many sane, straight guys who wouldn't have some kind of physical reaction if a lush female body was pressed against them. Not that she was actually *pressed* against him...

Alec sighed and tried to force his thoughts in a different direction. AJ's breathing was soft and almost even, and there was no doubt her earlier pain had lessened somewhat, at least in sleep. Taking a chance, Alec shifted positions, hoping to at least get a little more comfortable, if not away from the bed altogether.

AJ moaned as soon as he moved, another whimper of vulnerability. Her hand twitched for a brief second then came to rest on his thigh, just at the hem of his shorts. Alec groaned himself then clenched his jaw.

It was going to be a very long night.

#

AJ squeezed her eyes tighter against the light she could sense trying to intrude on her and rolled onto her stomach. The sharp pain from last night was gone, replaced by a dull throb that was so much more bearable. She swallowed, grateful that the migraine had been a minor one.

Probably due in part to the medicine Alec had given her. She remembered him coming into her room sometime last night. She would have to thank him—

AJ's whole body stiffened as bits and pieces of last night came back to her. What had happened after Alec had given her the pills? She remembered feeling someone stroke her hair away from her face, remembered feeling the comfort of arms around her...

AJ opened her eyes, honestly afraid of what she would find. She turned her head to the side and her heart stopped.

A pair of deep, dark brown eyes stared back at her, so close that she could see the flecks of gold in them and the line of darker brown that ringed the irises. The intensity in their depths unnerved her, and not just because they were mere inches away.

AJ swallowed. The action kick-started her heart into overdrive, and for a brief second she thought she might actually start to hyperventilate. But she didn't move. She couldn't: she was held in place by the intense study of those eyes.

"How are you feeling?" Alec's voice was a husky whisper in the grayness of the room, hypnotic with the warmth of the words.

AJ nodded, not trusting her voice. And still Alec studied her, as if he was trying to decipher some secret. She finally lowered her eyes in an attempt to escape the heat of his gaze, and immediately wished she hadn't.

Alec was stretched out next to her, so close she could feel the heat of his body even though he was lying on top of the sheet that covered her. Her eyes took in the sight of his half-naked body. A generous sprinkling of hair covered his tanned and muscled chest, just enough for someone to tease with their fingers. The dark hair tapered down to a narrow line that disappeared into the waist band of the gym shorts he had on last night...gym shorts that may have been loose but not so loose that she didn't notice...yeah, he was definitely very nicely built—all over.

AJ swallowed against the dryness in her mouth and quickly averted her eyes, afraid he would catch her staring. She glanced back up at him to see that he was still watching her, his face carefully blank. She had the sudden urge to reach out and touch the heavy growth of stubble along his jaw line, just to see how it would feel against her palm.

But AJ didn't move, she just lay there frozen and hoped that her thoughts weren't written all over her face. It didn't help that Alec still hadn't so much as twitched a muscle. He was so still that he could be carved from stone.

"I have practice in a little bit. Do you feel up to going or would you rather stay here?"

"Uh...I...I can go."

"Okay."

She expected Alec to get out of the bed, to leave her room and get ready. At the very least, she thought he would move away but he didn't. Not like she expected.

He reached out with one hand and brushed a strand of hair away from her eyes. The gentle touch came close to snapping something inside her, and it was only for fear of embarrassment that she didn't move an inch. AJ gave herself credit for not leaning forward just the tiniest bit—that's all it would take for her lips to brush his. The thought sent heat spiraling through her and her gaze dropped to his lips. Firm, fuller than she first realized, well-sculpted like the rest of him.

More thoughts whirled through her mind in those few

seconds: what his lips would taste like, what his tongue would feel like as it danced in her mouth and over her skin...

AJ bit back on the moan in her throat and forced herself to stare at the wall, knowing there was no doubt Alec could see her blush. Her face was so warm, she was surprised he couldn't feel it as close he was.

Or maybe he did. He suddenly chuckled then rolled out of the bed in one swift move that reminded her of his agility on the ice. Surprised, she looked up and found him smiling down at her, his eyes alight with mischief. He braced his weight on one hand as he leaned over her, so close again that she thought he really was going to kiss her.

"The next time I'm in your bed, neither one of us will be doing any sleeping!" The words were barely a whisper, the teasing clear in their tone. AJ gasped both in shock and indignation. How dare he?

She was ready to make some sarcastic retort when she noticed the heat in his dark eyes and realized that while his words might be teasing, he was serious about his intent. Her jaw snapped shut as images of their naked bodies rubbing against each other, learning, teasing, pleasing, came to mind. She may have squeaked in surprise, or worse, moaned in anticipation, but before she could cover it, Alec straightened, reached out and swatted her backside playfully, then walked out of the room without another word.

SIX

Alec swore as the puck rushed past his glove and hit the post with a clang before falling into the net. Part of him wanted to rip his gloves and helmet off in frustration, to throw them to the ice and kick them in a fit of temper. He barely resisted the temptation.

Barely.

The only thing stopping him was knowing that his teammates would look at him even more strangely than they had been throughout the entire practice. If not for the fact that he had a visitor, he'd walk off the ice and call it quits for the day.

But that wasn't an option. And every time he looked up, he noticed that his visitor wasn't even paying any attention to him. For some reason, that bothered him. Shouldn't she be as aware of him as he was of her?

But no. Every time he glanced to where she was sitting in the stands, she was engrossed in something. He could see her fingers typing furiously at the keyboard of the laptop she dragged with her. Another time she was engrossed in a deep conversation on her cell phone. The one time he thought she might have been watching, he actually stopped what he was doing and looked up at her. It wasn't until the puck clipped the side of his leg as it flew past him that he realized she wasn't watching him at all, she was staring off into space.

The lack of attention wasn't bad just for his concentration, it was killing his ego. His mind had been focused on one thing and one thing only ever since he woke up next to her this morning. Did she even remember how she had curled against him while he held her in the middle of the night? How she had draped her body across his? It had taken all of his control—more than he thought he had—not to push the hem of her shirt up past her waist and run his hands along the silky smoothness of her skin. He had wanted nothing more than to wake her with kisses, to tangle his hands in her thick hair and ravage her, to feel her body come awake under his touch.

Alec moaned at the sudden discomfort gripping his groin then cursed beneath his breath as yet another puck clipped him, this time on his shoulder. A shrill whistle pierced the chilly air of the practice rink and he looked up to see Sonny LeBlanc storming across the ice toward him. More than a dozen sets of eyes were focused on him, including startling blue ones from up in the stands. Alec groaned again. Of course AJ would pick now to notice him.

The coach slid to a stop in front of him, showering him with ice from his skate blades. Alec straightened and lifted his helmet, bracing himself for the verbal assault he knew was coming.

Sonny stared at him for several long minutes. The silence was deafening, drawn out until Alec had to fight the urge to look away. With a quick motion of one hand, Sonny signaled the end of practice. Wordlessly, the other players skated from the ice as Sonny continued to stare at him. When there was no one left, the coach leaned forward and spoke in a voice pitched so low there was no possibility of anyone overhearing.

"Either sleep with her, Kolchak, or don't bring her to practice again. Hear me?"

Alec's jaw dropped at the blunt words. He snapped it shut then opened his mouth to say something, what he didn't know, but was stopped by a quick shake of Sonny's head.

"Don't say anything. It's obvious where your mind is. The team doesn't need it right now. What they need is you focused on your game." Sonny paused and looked toward the stands, then shook his head. "Do what you have to, but get back in your game."

Alec watched the coach skate away, still stunned into silence. He finally looked up into the stands, expecting to see AJ watching him. He clenched his jaw in frustration as he saw her typing away again on her laptop.

"But she's a freaking reporter," he muttered to himself. A reporter he had slept with. Last night was undoubtedly the most intimate night he had ever shared with a woman, at least in recent memory, and he doubted if she even remembered it. Oh, there was no doubt she had been affected by him this morning. He had seen it on her face, in the shy glances she had grazed his body with, in the faint blush that had bloomed across her cheeks. But that was completely different; Alec doubted if she even realized how intimate the night had been for him.

How could she? Even now, she was up in the stands, oblivious, immersed in whatever she was typing. The worst part was that he realized whatever she was writing, it was undoubtedly about him. That's what she had been after, right?

The thought left him chilled even as his body heated from the memory of her curled against him.

And suddenly Alec wanted to call the whole bet off. It had been a stupid idea. Not even twenty-four hours had passed and already his entire world had been turned upside down. He had no idea what she was writing and a part of him didn't want to know.

With a loud curse, Alec threw his stick and watched it slide across the ice until it crashed against the boards. He looked back to where AJ sat in the stands, watching him. Their eyes met for a brief moment before he looked away and skated off the ice. He didn't have to see her to know she had gone back to typing.

#

AJ chanced a sideways glance at Alec. His eyes were focused straight ahead, concentration—or something else—creasing his brow. His left arm rested against the door rest of the oversized, jacked-up truck while he drove with his right hand. Every few seconds or so, he would clench the leather-wrapped steering wheel—at about the same time his jaw would clench. Even if it hadn't been obvious by his expression and body language, she would have been able to tell something was wrong by the palpable tension that surrounded him. And as much as she wanted to, she had avoided asking him what was wrong for the last thirty minutes.

Her control wavered then finally snapped when he turned into the parking lot of the newspaper office with a squeal of tires. With her right hand still bracing herself against the dash, she turned in her seat and fixed Alec with what she hoped was a lethal stare.

"Just what, exactly, is your problem?"

Alec returned her stare with one of his own. But where she knew her eyes were cold, his were fiery, anger and impatience burning bright in their dark depths. His lips thinned for a split-second as he watched her, then relaxed only enough for his jaw to clench. A slight tic pulsated along his jaw line, removing any idea that AJ might have had that he was only a tad bit upset about anything but her.

Oh no, he was definitely more than just a *tad bit* upset. And it was definitely aimed right at her.

She sat up straighter, clenching her own jaw as she met his gaze straight on. "Do you want to tell me what it is I did that pissed you off so much, or am I just supposed to guess?"

"What were you typing at practice?"

The simmering anger in his tone distracted her for a few seconds before the actual words registered in her mind. She blinked, hard, not really believing she had heard him right. But she wasn't hearing things, wasn't imagining things.

"You've got to be kidding me." It was the first thing that popped out of her mouth, which was at least a little better than the sarcastic "Excuse me?" she wanted to say.

Apparently Alec didn't agree with her. He leaned toward her, so close that mere inches separated them, so close she could feel the heat radiating from his body. "What were you writing, AJ?"

She stared at him, studying him for a few quiet seconds as she tried to mentally peel through his anger. And suddenly it hit her: he wasn't angry, he was worried.

Why on earth would Alec Kolchak be worried about what she was writing?

Well, okay, so maybe she could understand a little bit of worry. He never gave interviews, ever. To suddenly have to give her one...and be stuck with her on top of it...had to stick in him at least a little. And all because he lost a bet because she actually scored on him...

And then there was that stupid article from a few years ago that had her name attached to it. Never mind that she didn't have a thing to do with it, nobody ever believed that...

A hot flame of anger surged through her but she quickly doused it. She absolutely *refused* to let that fiasco play a part in who and what she was today. It was behind her.

"What were you writing, AJ?" Alec repeated the question, his voice flat and chilly. She swallowed once, twice, trying to rein in her anger and disappointment.

So maybe it wasn't as far behind her as she thought.

AJ sighed, leaving no doubt about how furious she was in the sound, and shoved open the truck door. Pulling her backpack off the seat as she jumped out, she fixed Alec with as cold a glare as she could manage.

"I was writing about how big an ass you are!"

She slammed the door as hard as she could, gratified at his groan as the truck frame shook with the force. Let him take that, she thought, storming toward the building. It would serve him right if she *had* been writing about his being an ass. Too bad she wasn't that vindictive. The funny thing was, she hadn't even been writing about him. Not really.

Because she had been entirely too distracted by the memory of waking up with him in bed next to her. She paused before pulling open the door, taking a deep breath and willing the heat in her face to fade. She was about to tell Tim that her crazy idea worked, and that she was going to get the interview. The last thing she needed was for him to sense something else was going on...like this sudden irrational attraction to Alec.

#

Alec glanced at his watch then jammed the power button of the truck's stereo. Twenty minutes had passed already...what could AJ be doing in there for that long? She said all she had to do was run in and get something...

What if she was doing more than getting something? What if she was already turning in her article? Clenching his jaw in frustration, Alec got out of the truck and walked into the building. It wasn't too difficult to find the correct floor, and the elevator ride up was brief enough. Not so brief that his anger didn't have time to grow, which he knew was irrational but didn't bother to stop anyway.

The elevator doors opened with a soft hiss. Alec wasn't sure what he had been expecting, maybe a scene like something from one of the many television sitcoms. The controlled quiet that greeted him was surprising.

He stepped off the elevator and looked around. A central reception area was just ahead of him, with cubicles laid out in a maze on either side of a main aisle. Wood-and-glass encased offices flanked the rear of the floor.

Right now the reception area was empty. Muted voices and assorted noises drifted from the maze of cubicles, their owners hidden behind the fabric-covered portable walls. Alec looked around, searching for AJ, then started walking past cubicles, ignoring the curious glances as he peered into each one as he passed. Laughter caught his attention and he turned in time to see her stepping out of one of the offices, her profile turned to him as she continued talking with whoever was in the office.

Alec noticed a subtle stiffening in her posture a half second before she turned toward him. A flare of impatience erupted inside him, quick and irrational, as the laughter faded from her eyes. He watched as she stood there in uncertainty, their gazes locked for the briefest moment. His eyes drifted to her mouth as she pulled on her lower lip with her teeth, and he suddenly remembered Sonny's earlier comment: *Sleep with her.* That was quickly followed by the memory of her body curled against his, soft and flush with sleep.

Something must have shown on his face, because AJ's expression quickly turned to one of bewilderment. Her brow furrowed for a quick instant before she turned her attention away from him, apparently listening to whoever was in the office. She shot a quick look back at Alec, another to the invisible speaker, then back to Alec. Her body language screamed that she would rather have him leave, but she motioned him forward instead.

Alec closed the distance to the office, only partially aware of the stares following him as he focused more on AJ's face. There was something in her expression, a look in her eye that he didn't quite understand. Was he imagining things, or was she warning him about something?

He stopped next to her, still studying her, watching the blue of her eyes darken even as she reached for his arm and yanked him into the office. "Alec, this is Tim Norton, my editor. Tim, meet Alec Kolchak."

Alec pulled his gaze away from AJ and turned in the direction she was motioning, only to find himself being studied by a set of narrowed eyes peering from behind thick-rimmed glasses. A rapid tat-tat-tat of a pencil tapping against the desk echoed in the otherwise quiet room as Tim continued to study him. A long minute passed before the narrow-eyed gaze shifted to AJ.

"Close the door, AJ." The request was issued quietly, but with enough authority that AJ quickly complied. Tim stood and walked around the desk, leaning against the edge as he folded his arms across his chest and looked at both of them. "Is anything going on here that I need to know about?"

Alec wouldn't have known right away what the comment meant if not for the flush coloring AJ's cheeks. As soon as the insinuation sunk in, he stood straighter and took a step forward. He was stopped by Tim holding a placating hand in his direction, accompanied by a raised eyebrow.

"Easy, son. I'm not implying anything, just asking a question." The editor turned his gaze to AJ. "Gerry Brown came charging in here yesterday—"

"Oh, great. I can just imagine what that asshole—"

"AJ, enough. If you're serious about this, you have to stop letting people like Gerry Brown get to you. It's seen as a weakness, and as soon as any of these sharks—including me—see a weakness, it's a feeding frenzy and you know it."

AJ's jaw tightened, her entire posture stubborn and defensive. It was so completely different from her reactions around Gerry Brown that Alec wondered why the asshole had such a negative effect on her. He watched her for a few more minutes, finally relaxing his own guard a bit when he noticed the stubborn lift of her chin settle.

"So you were saying?"

Tim shook his head, just a small movement as he lips lifted into a small, brief small.

"I do like your style, AJ, you know that." He moved back behind his desk, sitting in the chair with a creak. "Gerry was extremely glad to let me know that you propositioned our hockey player here in order to get an interview."

"That's—" She was interrupted by Tim's quick hand motion.

"Semantics. After questioning him, I was given the details of your proposition. He also admitted he had been given the same chance but didn't take it. That I would have liked to see." Another brief smile lifted one corner of his mouth before he focused his attention squarely on Alec. The sudden intensity caught Alec off-guard, especially since he had felt invisible right up to that moment. "So, Mr. Hockey Player...my girl actually scored a goal with you in the net, huh?"

Now it was Alec's turn to flush, a disconcerting feeling, especially since he had just been made to feel as if his athletic abilities had been called into question. He opened his mouth for what surely would have been a stammered reply but was interrupted by AJ.

"It was a lucky shot, trust me. I fell on the ice and slid straight into him. The only reason the puck crossed the line is because he was more worried about me plowing into him."

Tim flicked his gaze between the two of them, watching. Alec was barely aware of the scrutiny because his attention was focused on AJ. She stood with a feigned casualness, her gaze forced straight ahead on the wall behind Tim. Alec cleared his throat.

"Actually, it was a pretty decent shot and I wasn't expecting it. I have no idea if I would have stopped it even if she hadn't, you know...slid...into me." Alec couldn't believe he had just admitted that. From the look AJ was now giving him, she couldn't believe it, either. What the hell had just gotten into him that he would ever admit that?

"Hmm. Regardless..." Again, Tim divided his gaze between him and AJ, accompanying each glance with a tap, tap, tap of his pencil. "I don't care about any physical relationship you two have. What I need to know is if it's going to get in the way of this interview."

"Excuse me?" Alec's remarkably controlled response was much tamer than AJ's outburst.

"That's bull, Tim! There is no relationship. Trust me. Especially not physical—"

"AJ, I am not blind, even if you two are. And I don't really care what goes on behind closed doors. But make sure it stays there. Be discreet. Any hint of indiscretion is going to taint whatever article comes out of this. You don't want to lose this opportunity over something like a sexual indiscretion."

Alec was stunned into speechlessness. Even if he had known what to say—and his mind was completely, unforgivably blank—he wouldn't have been able to utter a single word.

"Gee, Tim, thanks for the vote of confidence. Thanks for thinking I would stoop so low as to trade sex for a story. Unfreaking-believable. You know, you rank right up there with Gerry. Worse, because I thought—"

"AJ, save your breath. I don't think that. But you know how this business works. You don't need something like that tied to your name."

"Yeah, whatever."

"AJ..."

She shook her head and gave her editor a 'talk to the hand' gesture. "Don't even. I don't want to hear it."

A long silence stretched around them, but still not long enough for Alec to think of anything to say. He stood there, in the middle of the room, feeling like an outsider despite the fact that he was very much a prominent subject of the conversation.

But I don't even like her. The thought crossed his mind, followed by swift denial. He did like her. He'd been thinking just this morning—hell, just two hours ago!—what it would be like to be tangled in the sheets with her, her luscious curves draped around him, her long hair caressing his bare skin—

"Oh for crissakes, Kolchak. Give me a break. You're as bad as Tim. I'm out of here."

Alec watched in bewilderment as AJ stormed out of the office. Had he missed something?

A chuckle pulled his attention back to the man seated behind the desk.

"Don't ever play poker, son. Everything you're thinking is written clear as day on your face."

"Shit. And people wonder why I hate reporters." Alec turned and skulked out of the office, wondering what the hell he was supposed to do now.

SEVEN

AJ breathed in deep, held it, and tried like hell not to let it out in a rush but God, it hurt. She would *not* look at him, would *not* let him see her struggle, would *not* look at him—

The weights crashed down with a loud bang, which at least hid the sound of the breath rushing out of her as she grunted in both pain and exasperation. *This* is why working out was unnatural.

"You okay?" Alec barely spared her a glance as he effortlessly raised and lowered the weights against his chest.

His bare chest.

Double damn, she looked.

She mumbled a reply, afraid that her voice would sound anything but calm and collected. It took a lot more concentration than she would have thought necessary to control her breathing, to take slow, measured breaths instead of gulping in air. Sweat dripped down the sides of her face and she had to resist the urge to reach up and press her shirt against her chest in order to stop the trickle of sweat dripping between her breasts. Her pulse pounded, and she swore to herself that it had absolutely nothing—*nothing*—to do with the fact that Alec Kolchak was less than five feet away from her, half-naked, buff, and gleaming in the fluorescent lights.

Her arm muscles quivered and her legs felt like jelly, and there was no way *that* was from watching the play of Alec's muscles as he continued his bench presses.

Nope, she was not affected in the least by the smooth motion of his arms as he lifted up, down, up, down...as the bar came so close to that sculpted chest, as his muscles stretched and contracted with each movement. She was *not* captivated by the sight of his sculpted jaw, covered in dark stubble; she was *not* fascinated by his full lips and how they quirked with each breath he took in and let out.

Nope. She was *not* sneaking looks at him as he laid back, stretched out on the bench, his abs so tight and defined that she wanted to reach out and touch them, feel if his skin was warm over all that muscle. She did *not* want to reach out and trace the thin line of hair that disappeared into the waistband of his loose gym shorts.

And she absolutely was *not* remembering the look he gave her the other day in Tim's office. The look that had started out vaguely confused then quickly morphed into one of smoldering liquid heat. Aimed at *her*.

God, what was she supposed to think about *that*? The look had caught her so completely off-guard that at first she was stupefied into silence. Then, as the heat from his gaze seeped into her, warming her from inside out, her mouth came to life.

Of course, that *would* happen seconds before her brain kicked in. She was an idiot. She couldn't remember her exact words, but she knew they were stupid and exasperating. And then she just turned around and left. Walked out. No sassy comeback, no sexy retort, no whimsical reply. Just idiocy and...escape.

Alec had looked at her with heated desire deep in his eyes. After sleeping with her the night before. After taking care of her. After wrapping his arms around her and comforting her. After sleeping in the same bed with her!

Which meant absolutely nothing. But still...she could have come up with something a little wittier than whatever stupidity stumbled from her mouth.

Only now, she was beginning to wonder if she had imagined the whole thing. Alec had followed her out of the office only minutes later, and there was no indication on his part that there had been any look of any kind. He was back to being the quiet, reserved, grumpy guy he usually was around her.

Which was just as well, because no matter what half-baked fantasy was trying to form in her mind, there would be absolutely nothing happening between them. This article—this story, and her chance for the column, her chance at redemption—could not be tainted in any way. And after Tim's comments the other day...

"It actually works better if you move the weights with your legs, instead of scowling at them."

AJ shook her head and turned to find Alec standing less than a foot away. Her mouth went suddenly dry and her mind went completely blank. With the way she was reclined on the leg press, with the way Alec was standing, her eyes—mouth—was directly level with...

She snapped her gaze upward as her face heated to a hundred degrees, and she absolutely refused—*refused*—to let her eyes rest anywhere other than on his own amused gaze. A few dozen retorts came to mind but she bit down on all of them. Looking away, she gritted her teeth and pressed down so hard with her legs she thought the weights should go flying across the room. Instead, they barely moved.

She heard Alec chuckle as he put distance between them, and she wondered if that had been a deliberate move on his part, if he had stood like that, so close, on purpose. Maybe if she ignored him, if she pretended he wasn't there...

But she knew better. That was never going to happen, not when his presence literally surrounded her whenever he was near. She didn't even have to see him enter a room—she just knew, could just feel it.

And really, when had that started? When had she become so hyper-aware of him as a man instead of just a player, another story? At the rate she was going, she'd have him elevated to god-status before she could think of more words to write.

AJ grunted as her legs pressed out then slowly squeezed back. *More* words to write. That was almost laughable, since nothing she had come up with so far was working. There was one large file with deleted material, and one miniscule file. With a title...and nothing much more.

Because no matter how hard she tried, she couldn't come up with the right angle. Everything fell flat. Lackluster. Boring. Why was it so hard to capture the essence of Alec on paper?

She stole a glance at him and had to quickly swallow a gasp of surprise. He was standing right at her feet, watching her with intent eyes. The weights crashed against each other as her legs gave out and she gritted her teeth.

"Why do you do that? Why do you have to sneak up on me like that?"

Alec chuckled and shook his head. "I did not sneak up on you—you just weren't paying any attention. Guess you finally found your zone, huh?"

Zone. Yeah, she had found it alright...but it had nothing whatsoever to do with the workout Alec was forcing on her.

"You ready for a break?"

AJ nodded and quickly slid off the machine, wincing as a spasm raced through her right thigh. She brushed off the feeling and stepped away from Alec's reaching hand, knowing that he must think she was an absolute, graceless klutz prone to accidents and mishaps.

"A break, huh? For what? Five minutes until Round Six of today's torture session?" AJ hadn't said it to be funny, but he laughed anyway, turning the lights off as they left the gym and headed down the hallway. She eyed the stairs dubiously, pausing behind Alec as he went down them, and wondered if her rubber band legs would survive the descent.

The only positive thing that would come of her falling is that she'd take Alec down in her tumble.

With that cheery thought, she took first one step then another, mentally grimacing with each one.

"No more torture. We'll each have a protein shake, wash up real quick, then hit the hot tub."

AJ paused mid-step and almost did stumble. Hot tub? She had to be hearing things. There was no way—*No. Way.*—she was going to get into a hot tub with Alec.

"And don't say no. With the way you're moving now, if you don't do something to ease those muscles, you'll be stiff as a board before midnight, and completely miserable tomorrow."

AJ still didn't move, didn't even blink as Alec turned and looked up at her from the bottom step. She was already miserable, and it was all his damn fault for the obstacle course of activities he had been putting her through for the last several days. It wasn't even six o'clock at night and she was ready to crash face-first into her bed.

But as much as she wanted to protest, AJ kept her mouth shut. She knew Alec had a plan, and that plan was to get rid of her. It was relentless torture designed to make her give up.

Gritting her teeth, she walked the rest of the way down the

steps. Alec wasn't going to win that easily.

#

She stood in the hall just outside the door to Alec's bedroom, not quite sure if she could actually cross the threshold. Yes, she knew she wasn't actually going *into* his room—technically she was just passing through it.

To get to the hot tub. On the balcony.

Which was worse than actually going into his room.

AJ took a deep breath, working up her nerve even as a large part of her—a very large part—was ready to turn tail and hide. Or better yet, just run away.

Except that would make her a coward.

Gritting her teeth, she reached for the door knob and turned it, pushing open the door and stepping into the room before she could chicken out. She refused to look at the large bed off to the side of the huge room.

But seriously, how big a bed did one person really need? The thing was huge. It had to have been custom-made, sitting on an elevated platform, made up in luxurious shades of deep blues. AJ yanked her gaze from the bed and kept walking across the room, one foot in front of the other, heading toward the French doors that opened onto the balcony.

She stopped again, her gaze taking in the breathtaking view of the harbor, the pinpoints of light from the Baltimore skyline reflecting on the calm surface of the water stretched out eight stories below. Despite the activity and bustle that she knew was going on down there, it was quiet and peaceful from this private haven. Almost serene.

Until she turned and got a good look at the massive hot tub and nearly turned tail to run again.

It wasn't the actual hot tub that scared her. As big as it was, eight people could fit in it without even touching each other. No, it definitely was not the hot tub that scared her.

It was the man sitting in it.

Alec was stretched out, his arms draped along the sides, a beer bottle held loosely in one hand as his head leaned back against a built-in cushion. Bubbling water foamed around him, reaching midchest, steam caressing his sculpted body as a look of pure masculine contentment radiated from his face. AJ's mouth went dry as she stared at him, feeling safe for at least a few seconds since his eyes were closed and he couldn't see her.

"Are you going to stand there all night or are you going to get in?" His voice had a hollow quality to it as it mixed with the sound of the rolling water and drifted away with the steam. AJ bit back her squeal of surprise then hesitantly took a step toward the tub. "There's beer in the small refrigerator over there if you want one."

She paused mid-step and looked off to the side. Sure enough, there was a refrigerator. Right next to the small wet bar. She changed direction and headed to the fridge, opening it up and pulling out an icy bottle.

"Would you mind getting me another one?" She heard him shift in the tub behind her, heard water slosh as he changed positions as she grabbed a second bottle. "What the hell are you wearing?"

AJ straightened abruptly, both bottles held tightly in her hands as she turned around to face him. He was staring at her in wide-eyed surprise, the steam doing little to block the intensity of his gaze. She looked down at her black t-shirt and running shorts then back up at him.

"What's it look like I'm wearing?"

"You have a bathing suit on under that, don't you? I mean, you're not planning on getting in here dressed like that, right?"

AJ had been walking toward the hot tub but abruptly stopped, just close enough to hand Alec his beer. He leaned out to take it, treating her to a nice glimpse of bare chest and bare abs and...

"Are you naked?" Her mouth clamped shut as the words left her, and she wished she could take them back, especially after the look Alec gave her. He twisted the cap off the bottle and tossed it to the side, then took a deep swig and stood up, his arms held out to the side. AJ swallowed back her disappointment when she saw the loose swim trunks sitting low—really low—around his lean hips.

"No, I'm not naked. I'm wearing swimming trunks. Which, by the way, are the only two options for a hot tub so I hope you have a bathing suit on under that outfit." He lowered himself back into the hot tub, his back partially turned to her, his eyes closed as he rested his head against the cushion.

She stood at the edge of the tub, chewing on her lower lip in indecision. Yes, she had a bathing suit on underneath. A bikini. A simple black bikini, with two ties for the top and two ties for the bottom.

What she wanted to have on was a solid, lead-lined sturdy one-piece. Or a wet suit. She thought she might even actually prefer wearing a suit of armor and drowning over getting into a hot tub with Alec wearing nothing but a bikini.

"Coward." The word was a mocking accusation, a teasing dare issued in a voice just above a whisper. AJ gritted her teeth, then sat her beer down and pulled off the t-shirt and shorts.

"You're an ass," she grumbled as she leaned over for her beer then hoisted herself onto the edge of the hot tub and swung her legs to the side. She heard Alec chuckle and knew he was laughing at her, then the chuckle turned to a slight choking sound, as if he had swallowed his beer the wrong way.

She refused to look at him, just lowered her legs into the steaming water, her body following. A sigh of contentment escaped her and she sunk lower onto the built-in bench, the water lapping around her shoulders as she leaned back. Keeping her eyes closed, she raised the bottle to her lips and took a sip of the cold beer, then rested her head against the side.

The sensation was delicious, relaxing, serene. Her muscles relaxed instantly; the tension flowed outward from her limbs and slowly disappeared, leaving behind a deceptive calm. AJ breathed in deeply and melted into the water, losing herself.

"Feel better?" Alec's voice came to her from far-away, sounding almost hollow, swallowed amid the steam and frothing bubbles surrounding them. She nodded, having only enough energy to take another sip of beer.

Minutes drifted by as AJ's body relaxed even more, as all thought, stress, and worry were washed away by the steaming water. She felt herself sink lower, the water now lapping around her neck. There was a tug on her beer bottle and her hand instinctively tightened around it, pulling it back. Her eyes fluttered opened and she sucked in a deep breath as her eyes met Alec's, less than a foot away. His hand was clasped over hers, anchoring the bottle in her hand. She straightened and pulled away, just a few inches, just until he released his hold on her.

"Just making sure you weren't falling asleep." His eyes locked on hers, his expression steady, unreadable. She couldn't look away, even as she took several deep swallows from the bottle.

"I'm not." She drained the bottle, her eyes still held by his, her heart pounding at the expression in his gaze. She still couldn't read it and didn't understand it, and her nervousness suddenly increased.

AJ shifted and placed her empty bottle over the side, having to lean slightly out of the tub to sit it down. She could have sworn she heard Alec choke again, but when she turned to look at him, his eyes were closed, his head tilted back, his jaw clenched.

AJ decided to ignore him, to pretend he wasn't there, and allowed herself to fully stretch out in the tub, secure in the knowledge that the hot tub was big enough that she wouldn't be in danger of touching him. The water flowed over her again and she sighed deeply, giving into the seductive call of the pulsating heated water.

There was a small splash and gentle waves, and she heard Alec climb out of the tub. He asked if she wanted another beer and she murmured yes, almost completely relaxed now, the aches in her body fading away, her mind gradually emptying of all thought.

She inhaled deeply and sunk even lower, then sucked in her breath as a stream of ice cold liquid hit the top of her head and streamed over her face. She sat up, sputtering, her eyes wide as Alec's laughter echoed behind her.

"Oh my God. Oh..." AJ turned and stood, stumbling along the edge of the hot tub as beer streamed down her face, dripping out of her hair and off her chin onto her chest. "Why did you do that? You...you..."

Still laughing, Alec pulled two beers from the refrigerator and walked back to the hot tub, neatly jumping over the side and sliding in with a splash. "Sorry, you looked too relaxed. I couldn't resist."

Still sputtering, she glared at him, ignoring the bottle in his outstretched hand. "I thought the whole point of this was to relax!"

"You're right. I'm sorry. Here." He motioned for her to take the beer again, but she shook her head.

"Forget it. I'm going to take a shower and go to bed." She pushed her beer-soaked hair out of her face and sloshed through the water to the edge, stopping as Alec reached for her arm, his face serious now.

"AJ...Amber, don't. I'm sorry. Really. C'mon, it's just beer, you can rinse it off right here." She stared up at him, at his dark eyes and full lips, at the look of contrition on his face. Then she stepped toward him and pushed against his chest with both hands, thinking she could catch him off-guard and send him falling into the water.

And it worked. At least partly. Because he did stumble backwards and begin falling, only he reached out for her as he went, wrapping his arms around her and taking her down with him. Her chest collided with his, their legs tangling together as they both went under the water.

Alec's arms tightened even more as he rolled with her under the water then pulled, finally resurfacing so he was sitting along the bench seat. AJ had instinctively wrapped her arms around his neck when they went under, and now found herself clinging to him, drawn across his lap, straddling him.

And she was pretty sure that wasn't a beer bottle wedged between them.

Alec's eyes darkened as he looked at her, neither of them moving, AJ barely daring to breathe. She knew she should move away, needed to move away, but she couldn't—she was pinned in place by not only his piercing look but by his hands at her waist, by his thumbs gently rubbing circles along her hips.

Other than that small movement of his thumbs against her skin, neither of them moved, neither of them said a word. Heat rose through her, from the water, from his touch, from the look in his eyes. And still she didn't move, caught in some hypnotic state of suspension, of anticipation. From somewhere in the back of her mind, a small voice of reason shouted to be heard, tried to tell her that she needed to say something, to move away, to run away before it was too late.

But it was already too late. Alec's hold on her tightened and he pulled her closer, his eyes still locked on hers as he lowered his head and gently, hesitantly touched his lips to hers for a sweetly electrifying and all too brief kiss.

EIGHT

Alec pulled back slightly, looking as dazed as she felt, as if waiting for her to say or do something. Again a small voice in the back of her mind screamed at her to run away, warned that this was a disaster waiting to happen, that there was still time to come to her senses before she crossed the line.

AJ ignored the voice and leaned forward, and the world around her erupted. Alec's mouth claimed hers with a hunger that fed her own, and she eagerly met him with a fierceness that took her breath away. His hands roamed over her, touching, caressing, a sensual mix of hot flesh and hot water against her skin. She pressed herself tighter against him, feeling the hard length of his erection between her legs, heat building inside her at the contact. She rubbed against him, needing to feel more of him, all of him...

Alec broke the kiss, his breathing harsh, his eyes locked on hers, his hand pushing back the wet strands of her hair. There was no sound except for the water around them, drowning out all other sound, including the heavy beating of AJ's heart. It had been just a kiss. How could she be as effected as she was by just a kiss? Alec looked as bewildered as she felt, as if he, too, was trying to figure out what had happened. They stared at each other in silence, their eyes locked, AJ's breathing becoming harsher as the heat grew between them.

Alec cupped her face in his hands, his dark eyes searching, his thumb caressing her lower lip and sending sparks shooting through her. Slowly, achingly, he leaned forward again, his mouth closing over hers with a tenderness that made her melt into him even more. She tightened her arms around his neck, her fingers playing in his hair as he deepened the kiss. One of his hands reached around and cradled the back of her head, the other skimmed her back, tracing a path down along her spine, stopping just below her waist, steadying her as he thrust upward with his hips, slowly, pressing his hard length against her.

She moaned, just the tiniest sound, but it seemed to be all he needed. His touch became bolder, his hands hot against her slick skin, igniting trails of fire everywhere he touched. He pulled his lips from hers and traced a path along her neck, along her collarbone.

AJ's breath rushed from her in a hiss, her head tilted back, her fingers digging into Alec's shoulders as his hands closed around her hips and pulled her closer, pressing her against him as his lips found hers again, as his mouth closed over hers, insistent, demanding. She ran her hands down his arms, feeling the hard muscle and warm flesh beneath her touch; ran her hands back up and over his shoulders, then down once more, her palms flat against the skin of his chest. His heart beat fast and steady against her palm, his muscles quivering beneath her touch as her hands drifted lower, following the thin line of hair down to his taut abs.

Alec pulled his lips from hers, his breath coming in harsh gasps, echoes of her own unsteady breathing. His gaze held hers as he dragged his hands up along her back, as he reached up and undid the ties of her bikini top. She pulled on her lower lip with her teeth as he hesitated, as if waiting for her to say no, waiting for her to stop him.

Or waiting for her to give him permission. She reached behind her and clasped her hand around his then gently tugged, pulling the ties loose as he laced his fingers with hers. The top fell away and she leaned against him, flesh to flesh, kissing him, their tongues mating in a wild frenzy.

Sensation washed over AJ, as hot and slick as the water of the hot tub. Alec's hands roamed over her, down her back, around to her front, cupping her breasts, kneading them, his thumbs gently teasing her hardened nipples into tighter peaks. She pressed herself further into his lap, his hips thrusting upward as she rocked against his erection. He reached behind her with one hand, sliding it downward and cupping her bottom as he slid forward off the bench, lifting her with him as he stood.

Her legs wrapped instinctively around him and she rocked against him once more, his arms holding her more fully against him as he turned and moved to the edge. Alec shifted forward ever so slightly, sitting her on the edge of the tub before he pulled away. She raised her arms to cover herself, suddenly self conscious, but he shook his head as he pushed her arms away.

"No. Let me look." His gaze roamed over her, heated and hungry, then slowly lifted upward and locked with hers. "You're beautiful."

His heated gaze drifted over her again, slow and lingering, igniting a feverish blush to her skin wherever he looked. Alec slowly leaned forward, his hands skimming over her body as his lips claimed hers, once more hungry, demanding, insistent.

AJ was breathless and on fire when he pulled away, his mouth trailing along her jawline and her neck, nipping her shoulder blade, lower until his mouth clamped over one nipple and sucked, twirling the hard peak with his tongue. She felt the pull deep inside her, felt an answering liquid heat form between her legs and she shifted, moaning, tangling her hands in his wet hair, holding him to her as her head fell backwards.

Alec moved to her other breast, treating her to more exquisite torture, gently easing her back until she was laying on the edge of the hot tub, her legs still submerged in the water, Alec kneeling on the bench between her knees.

His hands skimmed along her sides, his mouth following, lightly teasing her stomach, her hip bone as he undid the ties of the bathing suit bottom. He trailed kisses along the top edge of the material, his large hands caressing her thighs, behind her knees and her calves as he slid the material off her with his teeth.

AJ's breath caught in her throat and she gasped as the material fell away, exposing her, as his tongue traced a path down her wet center. Her hips arched into his mouth and he eased her legs apart, his hands touching, searching, teasing.

She reached out for him, her hands searching for purchase as her eyes fluttered, the lights from the stars and surrounding buildings flickering in her vision. Realization crept to the edge of consciousness and she tried to pull away, to sit up.

"Alec." Her voice was hoarse, breathless, and she had to clear her throat and try again. "Alec, stop. We're outside. Somebody could see us..."

He looked up at her, his gaze intense, holding hers, as he slid one finger slowly into her then back out, slid it in again. "I don't care."

A shiver spiraled through her at the look in his eyes, at the intensity of his gaze as he lowered his mouth to her, as his tongue stroked her clit, as he slid a second finger into her, deeper still, his eyes never leaving hers.

And the knowledge that somebody could be watching, coupled with his heated gaze, his tongue hard against her flesh, his fingers deep inside her, probing...sensations combined all at once and she exploded instantly, her back arching as a small scream escaped her, spasms rocking her body from deep inside her until she lost track of sight, sound, all sensation except for the feel of Alec between her legs.

A rush of water covered her, hot and pulsing, as arms wrapped around her, strong and supportive, and she realized that Alec had pulled her into the tub, was holding her close, his mouth covering hers in a demanding kiss as her body continued to spasm in his hold.

Seconds went by, minutes, as her senses slowly returned, as her body calmed. Alec gentled the kisses, his hands skimming across her flesh, cupping her bare bottom and pressing her gently against him, the material of his swimsuit rough against her skin, the hard shaft of his erection pressing against her belly.

"Alec..." His name was a soft moan against his mouth. She lowered her hand, trailing it down his chest and stomach, easing her fingers into the waist band of his trunks. His hand closed around her wrist, stopping her.

"AJ, oh God, don't. I don't think I can...holy shit..." She pushed his hand away and pushed at his shorts, freeing his erection, grabbing him in one hand and stroking him, slow and hard, from the base of his shaft all the way to the tip, silky hardness against her palm.

Alec's hands tightened at her waist, holding her still when all she wanted was to feel him against her. He closed his eyes and leaned his head back, his jaw clenched as she continued stroking him, squeezing even as she pushed forward until his back was against the side of the hot tub.

She knew what she wanted but didn't know how to ask, so she lowered her mouth to his and kissed him, then trailed her lips down his neck and chest until she disappeared under the water, keeping her mouth pressed against his body as she moved lower.

His hands closed over her shoulders as she ran her lips along his shaft, and he pulled her to the surface, crushing her against him even as a harsh laugh escaped him. "Oh God, you're going to drown trying that."

His words gave her the opening she needed, and she pushed against him, a shy smile on her face. "Then move so I don't have to drown."

His eyes darkened instantly, searching hers for a long second before he slowly raised himself on the edge of the tub and leaned back on his elbows, his erection hard and stiff in front of her. She kept her eyes glued to his as she rested her hands on his sides and pressed her lips to his chest, sliding down, following with her hands, down further still until she closed her mouth over him, twirling her tongue around the tip of his shaft then leaning forward to take in his length. A guttural growl escaped Alec's lips and his hands fisted in her hair as she sucked him, teasing, licking the entire length of him, pulling him into her mouth again. She reached out and cupped his sack in her hand, gently squeezing, teasing the base of his cock with her thumb as her mouth devoured him, in and out, hot and slick under her touch.

Alec's hands tightened in her hair, holding her head tightly, his hips thrusting, forcing his shaft deeper into her mouth as groans escaped him. AJ ran her hands along his hips and down his thighs, digging her fingers into the thick muscles of his strong legs, back up to his hips as she raised herself further from the hot tub, leaning over him, reveling in the taste of him, reveling in the pleasure she was giving him.

His hips thrust once more then his entire body stilled. His hands tightened around her, pulling her up, dragging her across his body until she was lying against him, his arms tight around her. His chest raised and lowered with each harsh breath, his eyes tightly shut, his jaw clenched. AJ leaned forward and dropped a kiss to his chest, dragging her fingertips across his flat stomach, reaching lower to hold him, stroke him, when his hand shot out and grabbed her wrist.

"AJ..." His voice was a harsh whisper, barely more than a hissing breath. He lay still, not moving for a full minute, then heaved a heavy sigh and opened his eyes, capturing her gaze with his. A dark look crossed his face and he pulled her roughly to him, his mouth crushing hers as he shifted, moving to a sitting position, cradling her in his arms. He swung his legs to the side and swiftly stood, lifting her with him, and she wrapped her arms tightly around his neck to keep from falling.

He strode across the balcony and into his room, their bodies dripping water as he walked toward the bed and eased her onto it. She lifted herself on one elbow, watching him, her heart stammering at the sight of his sudden intensity. He pulled open a nightstand drawer and rummaged through it, cursing under his breath until he pulled out a foil packet and ripped it open. Still standing, he sheathed himself with the condom then lowered himself next to her, turning so they were face-to-face. His hand reached out and stroked her cheek, tucking a strand of wet hair behind her ear, then cradling the back of her head in his palm and leaning forward to kiss her, deeply, intensely. AJ's stomach flipped and rolled in anticipation, her hands reaching up and gripping his broad shoulders as he rolled over her, resting the hard length of his erection between her legs, pressing gently against her opening.

He broke the kiss and looked down at her, fire in the darkness of his eyes as he searched her face. "You have no idea what you do to me, no idea how much I want you right now." His voice was harsh, and she imagined that he sounded not only determined, but confused as well. As confused as she felt, stunned by what had already happened, by what was about to happen.

She shook her head, not knowing what to say, and lifted her hips to meet his, to encourage him, welcome him. He groaned and dropped his head, his mouth closing over hers in a fierce kiss as his hands closed around her hips. He shifted her slightly under him, then drove his entire length into her in one fluid move. Her body arched under him, driving upward to meet him as a sigh of pleasure escaped her lips.

Heat built quickly inside her, a spontaneous rekindling of the earlier fire. Each thrust forced her closer to the edge, each stroke inside her, each touch of Alec's hands along her skin. He grabbed her hands and held them over her head, his dark eyes boring into hers before he leaned down and claimed her mouth, hungry and possessive. He thrust deeper into her, once, twice, and she exploded, shattering around him, her back arching, her hips grinding as his name was ripped from her lips.

Alec groaned and sat back on his heels, grabbed her hips and pulled her more tightly against him, his head tilted back as he thrust again. Again, harder, burying himself, a harsh groan signaling his own release.

Time stopped, silent except for long minutes of unsteady breathing. AJ's body slowly came back to itself, the pieces collecting and reassembling in the quiet semi-darkness. She reached out with one hand and smoothed it over Alec's damp chest, feeling his heart beating rapidly under her touch. He breathed, a heavy sigh, and gently lowered himself on top of her, moving slightly to the side, still buried inside her. His arms tightened around her and he lowered his head to her chest, his breathing deep and steady.

AJ curled one hand along the back of his neck and rested the other along his arm. A warm feeling of deep contentment flowed through her, a slight smile on her face as she drifted off to sleep, secure in Alec's hold.

#

Gray morning light filtered through the open curtains, casting the room in a shadowed glow. Sounds drifted in through the open balcony doors: noise of distant traffic, the faint wail of a siren, the shriek of a seagull floating somewhere over the water.

Alec stared up at the ceiling, one arm thrown over his head, the other curled across his chest. His breathing was steady but his mind was whirling in a thousand different directions, most of them having something to do with last night.

With the woman in bed next to him.

He turned his head slightly to the side and looked at AJ. She was sprawled on her stomach, her face turned away from him, hidden by both her arm and the tangled curtain of her hair. She had kicked the blankets off her sometime during the night, and was barely covered by a corner of the sheet draped precisely over the curve of her bare bottom.

His eyes drifted over her, from the curve of her skull partly buried in the overstuffed pillow, to her tanned arms and the graceful line of her back. They drifted lower, over her sheet-covered bottom that he now knew was all soft skin over firm muscle, down to the shapely length of legs that had wrapped so tightly around him last night.

His dick twitched and grew in response to both the sight of AJ's naked body so close to his as well as the memory of what their bodies had done together only hours ago. He silently swallowed his groan and turned his gaze back to the ceiling, trying to pull up images of train wrecks and car accidents and mass destruction, anything to banish the memory of last night and tame his fast-growing erection.

It wasn't working.

He was so screwed.

Minutes drifted by as different scenarios played through his head, all of them ending with him buried deep inside AJ's wet, tight warmth. None of them were a viable option, which meant his immediate future was holding either an extremely ice cold shower or self-gratification. Or both. Probably definitely both.

His dick twitched again, letting him know that neither option was particularly attractive. Alec swallowed another groan and closed his eyes.

"You don't have to smother yourself in the pillow. I know you're awake." His voice was hoarse, rusty-sounding, as if he hadn't used it in some time. Alec didn't bother clearing his throat and repeating himself, knowing that AJ had heard him. He felt her body stiffen, tense, but she didn't so much as twitch, not a single movement except for the rise and fall of her breathing.

He wondered what was going through her mind, what she was thinking. Judging from her absolute stillness, he'd bet it was a safe guess that she was having the same thoughts he was. That she was thinking last night had been a huge mistake. A mistake of mammoth proportions. The mother of all mistakes in the last few mistake-filled weeks.

So why the hell did that bother him so much?

He turned his head to look at AJ again, noting she still hadn't moved, that her face was still half-buried in the pillow and the curtain of her hair. "What? I didn't hear you."

She raised her head only slightly and he heard her blow hair out of her face, but she didn't turn to face him. "I said, would you go away so I can get up?"

Alec stared at her for a long second then resumed staring at the ceiling, his jaw clenched. "It's my bed." It was a stupid thing to say, juvenile and immature. Rudely inconsiderate. But her request had caught him off-guard, even stunned him. He was laying here with a raging hard-on, thinking only of burying himself deep inside her, and she wanted him to leave so she could get up?

She mumbled something into the pillow, and again he had to ask her to repeat it. This time when she lifted her head, she turned to face him, fire clear in her heavy-lidded blue eyes. "I said, some gentleman you are." She closed her eyes and turned her head away, then slowly pushed herself up to a sitting position and swung her legs over the side of the bed with a small groan.

Alec watched the swing of her hair against her back, watched the play of muscles in her arms and caught a glimpse of the full curve of her breast as she reached behind her and tugged on the sheet. She pulled harder, dislodging it from his waist and wrapping it around herself before she stood. He gritted his teeth as his hard-on stood even straighter, waving as if trying to get her attention.

No doubt about it, his body was a total traitor. And he was totally screwed.

She walked around the edge of the bed, going out of her way not to look at him. "I'm taking a shower. I smell like beer and hot tub and...I need a shower."

She had been going to say "sex". Alec knew it without a doubt. He closed his eyes, let out a heavy sigh. "AJ, I'm sor—"

"Don't you dare say it!"

The vehemence in her voice startled him. His eyes flew open and he pushed himself to a sitting position just as she straightened from picking something up off the floor. She had a pillow in her hand and threw it at him left-handed, her right hand still tangled in the sheet she was trying to cover herself with. Her feet got tangled in the excess length and she stumbled, quickly righted herself, and glared at him.

"I swear, Kolchak, if you even *think* about saying you're sorry, I'll...I'll...you'll regret it!" She stood a few feet away from him, her eyes blazing, her hair tousled around her face and shoulders, the ridiculous sheet wrapped haphazardly around her. Her chest rose and fell with each harsh breath, drawing his eyes downward—where they widened in alarm.

He pushed himself off the bed and reached her with one long stride, gently grabbing her elbow when she would have stepped away from him. He pulled her closer to him, out of the shadow, and straightened her left arm in front of him. There, ringing the soft flesh on the inside of her bicep, were four fresh bruises, each a little larger than a dime, overlaying the fading bruise from when she had fallen on the ice. He placed his hand along the marks and lifted her arm, finding a slightly larger bruise on the underside of her arm.

The marks fit his fingers perfectly.

Alec actually stumbled, feeling sick to his stomach at the sight of the marks marring her flesh. He dropped her arm and stepped back, raising his eyes to hers, waiting to see his own horror and condemnation reflected back at him.

Instead, AJ stood there looking at him as if he had lost his mind. He cleared his throat and motioned to her arm. "I'm sor...I didn't mean..."

"You're kidding, right?" She pulled the sheet more tightly around her then lifted her arm and looked at it before dropping it to her side. "Seriously? You're upset about this?"

"AJ, I marked you! My God, I actually hurt you!"

"Alec." Her voice was sharp, impatient. She blew out a deep breath and stared at him, different emotions playing across her face. "You did not hurt me. Last night. Nothing you did...we did...last night hurt me. We got a little...enthusiastic, that's all."

A blush crept across her cheeks and she looked away, embarrassed or ashamed, he couldn't tell. He was afraid to ask. She cleared her throat and lifted her eyes briefly to his, then lowered them again.

"Besides," she continued, motioning to his chest and lower, "you have some marks on you, too. So get over it, and don't you dare apologize. Because you did not hurt me. Last night."

AJ turned away from him, stumbling just a bit on the ends of the sheet, and walked out of the room, quietly closing the door behind her before he could think of anything to say. He knew, without knowing how, that he had just missed something, that there was something in her words or voice that he should have picked up but was missing.

Muttering under his breath, replaying her words in his mind, he walked into the bathroom and reached into the shower, turning the water on full blast to the hottest setting. Seeing the bruises on AJ's arm had taken care of his hard-on faster than anything else could have.

He turned and looked at himself in the mirror, his eyes widening briefly. AJ had said she wasn't the only one with marks, and he now understood. There were several scratches on his chest, as well as some small bite marks along his collarbone and the crook of his neck.

But it was the one lower that made him pause and suck in his breath. Tucked high on the inside of his thigh, damn near in the crease of his leg, exceedingly close to his balls. A clear reminder of where AJ's mouth had been.

Alec clenched his jaw tight and reached into the shower, turning the water to the coldest setting before stepping in.

NINE

Tap-tap-tap.

Tap-tap-tap.

Tim tossed the pencil onto his desk, leaned back in the chair with a loud squeak, tented his fingers under his chin, and stared at AJ. He was quiet for so long, his face completely blank, that she squirmed in the chair across from his desk, her hands fisting where she had them tucked under her legs.

"It's not an interview, AJ." His voice was flat, with no emotion in the tone at all. She leaned forward, ready to argue or at least defend herself, but Tim held up his hand to stop her. "It's better than an interview. I'm impressed."

AJ let out the breath she had been holding and sat back, the knots in her stomach slowly uncurling. She had had no idea how Tim was going to react to the article when she emailed it to him this morning, and had regretted sending it almost immediately. That regret had grown even larger when Tim called an hour ago and asked her to come in.

What had she been thinking?

Well, she knew what she had been thinking—the same thing she had been thinking for the last two days, and it had nothing to do with the article. It was pretty amazing that there even was an article, considering everything that had happened the last two days.

Which was, essentially, absolutely nothing.

Apparently waking up next to the world's biggest asshole after having the world's greatest sex ever with the same said asshole worked wonders for her writing. Although, to be fair, it wasn't like she had anything else to do for the last two days, since Alec had pretty much ignored her since that morning they woke up together.

In the same bed.

After having the world's greatest sex.

And yeah, she wasn't an idiot and knew it had been a mistake, knew that there wasn't anything more to it than two consenting adults getting together for one night. She knew that, knew not to read anything into it, knew not to expect anything from it, had even told herself that it would make things awkward for at least a little bit.

Yes, it would have been nice for at least a little bit of morning-after cuddle, but she hadn't expected that, either. What she really hadn't expected was Alec's aloofness and palpable regret filling the room with sub-zero temperatures before she was even fully awake. His attitude had been pure icy misery, as he held himself statue-still, laying as far away from her as he possibly could without rolling out of the enormous bed.

AJ still didn't know what was worse: that, or his attempted apology. Both memories still sparked anger, and she actually kicked the leg of her chair in retaliation to vent some of it.

Which made Tim sit back in his chair and stare at her. How had she forgotten where she was?

She knew how, and mentally kicked herself this time before looking over at Tim with a feigned wide-eyed innocence and gave him her complete attention.

"You haven't heard a word I said."

AJ opened her mouth to deny it, but wisely shut it. Tim shook his head then leaned forward, clacking away at his keyboard. "I like the entire set-up you've got going here, AJ. How much more do you have?"

"Um," she paused and looked away. More? Not much. As in, none.

Tim waved her off. "It doesn't matter. We can use what you've got so far. In fact, that would be even better for what I have in mind."

"In mind?" AJ sat up straighter now, worry flowing through her as she noticed the calculating gleam in Tim's eyes, the subdued excitement thrumming through him as he made notes on the post-it pad next to his computer, then clacked away again on the keyboard.

"Yeah. Forget the original interview idea. We're turning this into a feature series. Four parts, I think. We'll run this one on Sunday. I need the other installments by each Thursday. That gives you almost a full week to come up with the second one. Think you can handle that?" Tim pulled his gaze away from the computer long enough to look at her, the expression in his eyes actually taking her aback. Confidence, pride, encouragement. Tim had always been her mentor, had always believed in her, but seeing it so clearly now surprised her, and she wasn't sure why.

"Yeah, no problem." She forced more confidence into her voice than she felt, nodding her head enthusiastically.

"Excellent." He tilted his head and studied her for a second. "This really is great stuff, AJ. You should be proud. And don't be surprised when you're offered a full-time spot in four weeks. As far as I'm concerned, it's a done deal."

Done deal? Muted excitement and stunned disbelief filled her at the words. A four-week feature series and a full-time spot—exceedingly more than she had ever considered several weeks ago. AJ pushed herself out of the chair and mumbled an inane thanks to Tim then walked out the office, torn between skipping and stumbling. Tim liked her drivel, and what had started out as nothing more than some mindless musings about the game of ice hockey and one of its best goalies was now going to become the first part of a four-part feature that several hundred thousand people would read in three days' time.

AJ couldn't help it, she did a little skip as she entered the elevator and pushed the button for the lobby floor. She had set out to do something, and she was making it happen!

She couldn't believe it. A four-part feature. Read by thousands of people.

The elevator doors opened with a soft hiss and she stepped out, smiling as she thought of sharing the news with Alec.

She stumbled and the smile fell from her face as an icy blast tore through her.

Alec.

Oh my God, he was the last person she could share this with. The dead last. He would not be sharing her enthusiasm or excitement, she knew that as well as she knew her own name. But it wasn't like she couldn't *not* tell him—he would see it for himself in three days when it came out.

She had to tell him. She had to. She couldn't let him be blindsided by it. There was absolutely nothing in the article—the feature—that was even remotely negative or unflattering, but he still wouldn't like it. In fact, he would hate it.

She didn't want to think about how she knew he would hate it, didn't want to fool herself into thinking she actually knew him well enough to know how we would feel. But that didn't stop her from knowing.

Alec was going to hate it.

AJ pushed through the lobby doors, her excitement replaced by trepidation as she tried to figure out the best way to tell him when she got back to his place.

#

Alec stretched out on the oversized sofa and flipped through the channels on the remote, not seeing a single program that flashed across the large flat screen television. He wasn't channel surfing trying to find something to watch; he was channel surfing because he was trying to think of the best way to start the conversation he needed to have with AJ.

Yes, he *needed* to have the conversation. Not wanted—needed. Something had changed in the last two days, and not for the better. They had barely spoken to each other since the other morning, sharing little more than distantly polite exchanges.

For as much as he had hated the idea of spending time with her before the whole stupid bet had backfired on him, he thought that not having to deal with her incessant chattering would have been bliss.

Except she didn't really chatter, and certainly not incessantly.

But he still hadn't thought he would miss it, not really. His usually quiet house had always been his refuge, a place he could go to escape, to unwind, to just be himself. He enjoyed the occasional solitude, enjoyed just doing nothing, talking to no one. Unlike AJ, he didn't consider that hiding. It didn't matter that lately he had been feeling like something was missing. He wasn't hiding...he was enjoying his peace and privacy.

Except he hadn't enjoyed it the last two days. Instead of

being a welcoming quiet, the silence was oppressive.

He felt like his own house was condemning him.

So here he was, mindless channel surfing, trying to come up with a way to start a conversation with AJ, to make the last two days go away so he could hear her voice, her laughter, again.

Which was going to be hard as hell, considering the only thing he wanted to do every time he saw her was throw her against any flat surface, wrap her legs high around his waist, and bury himself deep inside her. He could just imagine *that* conversation.

Hey AJ...I really miss our talks. By the way, would you mind if I threw you against the wall and mindlessly banged you?

Christ.

The door opened behind him and he jumped, startled then guiltily when he looked over the sofa back and saw AJ walking in. She tossed her keys onto the hall table and took a few steps toward him. She stopped to look at him before completely entering the living room, her teeth pulling nervously on her lower lip.

Alec eyed her full mouth and swallowed a groan as memories from the other night raced straight to his groin. He pulled his gaze away from her lips and took in her outfit: a leather and shell necklace worn tight around her neck like a choker, a longer leather necklace with some kind of shell hanging from it, falling near the edge of a scalloped shirt that showed more cleavage than he thought she should be showing in public, especially when the longer necklace called attention to that same cleavage.

His gaze dropped lower still to her curve-hugging jeans with the slightly frayed patches hinting at the toned flesh of her thighs, the jeans tucked into brown boots. And shit, where did she get those boots? They looked like pirate boots, with a cuff around the top, the leather dark and soft, worn-looking like a bomber jacket. Except he didn't think many pirates wore boots with three-inch heels.

And suddenly Alec didn't want to talk. The only thing Alec wanted to do was find that flat surface he couldn't stop thinking about. Except that really wasn't going to work either, so he jumped from the sofa and took a step toward her, willing his mouth to start working, hoping the words would come out the right way.

"Alec, we need to talk."

Her words froze him in place, right in the middle of his tracks. They were words that nobody ever wanted to hear, no matter what the situation was. He couldn't read the look on her face, could only see that she really didn't want to talk about whatever it was she said they needed to talk about.

And suddenly he didn't want to talk. About anything. He held his hand out and shook his head, stopping her from saying anything else.

"We're going out. Just...give me five minutes and we'll leave."

"Alec—"

"Some of the guys are getting together tonight, so we'll go meet them and just hang out for a little bit."

"Alec—"

"Five minutes. Just stay there." He whirled around and headed for his room, taking the steps two at a time, thinking that a night out was suddenly a perfect idea.

#

AJ stared at the bright lights and flashing neon decorating the building in front of them in disbelief, then turned to face Alec to see if he was joking with her. He was too busy pulling the keys out of the ignition and putting his wallet in the back pocket of his jeans to notice her look. But he acted like nothing was out of the ordinary, and she couldn't tell if he was pulling her leg or not.

AJ didn't know what to think, considering how strange he had been acting since she had returned to his place a little more than an hour ago. He had almost literally dragged her out of his condo, brightly assuring her that a night out would be fun. Then, every time she had tried talking, he had interrupted, insisting they were going to have a great time, that this would be a perfect chance for her to get to know some of the other players.

Alec opened his door to get out, then seemed to finally notice that she was still seat-belted in and making no effort to move. He looked at her questioningly, and she pointed to the flashing neon in front of them.

"Um, Alec...you do know this is a strip club, right?"

She almost laughed at his expression, it was that comical. His head whipped from her to the building and back, his eyes momentarily widening before lowering in a frown. She couldn't be sure because of the light, but it almost looked like a blush was creeping across his face. His lips were moving and she knew he was muttering something, but she couldn't make out what it was as he dropped back into the driver's seat and closed the door.

"Shit, sorry. Wasn't thinking," he mumbled. He leaned back in the seat and jammed his hand into his front pocket, searching for the car keys. "Stupid. Stupid idea. No problem, we can go someplace else. Really, wasn't thinking and—"

"Alec." She reached out and closed her hand around his wrist to stop his digging for the keys. Her fingers brushed against his jeans and she quickly let him go, pulling her hand back to her own lap and clearing her throat. "Alec, it's no big deal. We can go in."

"What? Are you nuts? No, absolutely not. That would be— AJ, no, where are you going?"

She opened the door and stepped out, then turned and leaned into the car to stare at him. "I'm going inside." She straightened and closed the door then took a few steps across the parking lot, not surprised when Alec rushed up to her side and actually tried to stop her by stepping in front of her and walking backwards.

"AJ, you can't go in there. It's...it wouldn't be right."

She stopped a few feet from the door, hearing the bass of the pulsing beat of the music. "Why wouldn't it be right?"

"Uh...because it's a strip club and—"

"But it's okay for you guys?"

"Um..."

"No, this will be fun. C'mon." AJ pushed around him, trying not to smile at the look of surprise and chagrin on his face. She pulled open the door and felt the music wash over her, drowning out whatever Alec had been trying to say.

TEN

The small lobby was relatively well-lit, showing a glass counter of merchandise with assorted shirts and posters displayed on the wall behind it. A young blonde wearing what AJ thought was supposed to pass for a bikini was leaning across the counter, talking to one of the two bouncers. The second bouncer was standing in front of a doorway that was framed by a metal detector, a scowl on his dark face, beefy arms crossed in front of his massive chest. A gold hoop earring hung from his left ear, and his dark bald head sported some kind of tribal tattoo across the side. He looked like the kind of man that any sane person would run away from.

"Leon!"

"Oh my God, it's little Amber!" The big man stepped toward her then leaned down to wrap her in a tight bear hug. He swung her around, planting a kiss on the top of her head before setting her back on her feet. "What are you doing here, girl? You gonna finally get up on that stage for us?"

AJ stepped back, shaking her head and laughing. She couldn't see Alec behind her, but she was pretty sure he was frozen in place, probably with his mouth hanging open and a scowl on his face. "Oh no. Not me. I'm here with a friend, who's meeting some more friends."

Leon looked over her shoulder and scowled as Alec finally came to a stop next to her. She rolled her eyes as the two did that whole male sizing-up thing. "This here your friend, little Amber? Now you tell me, what kind of man brings a date to a strip club?"

AJ stepped toward Alec, stopping him from saying anything as she placed her hand on Leon's chest. "He's not my date, Leon. He plays hockey for the Banners, and I'm doing a story on him."

"Yeah? No shit. Well, there's more of them hockey players in the back." Leon stepped back and eyed Alec up, then dismissed him with a slight shake of his head and turned his attention back to AJ, a broad smile splitting his dark face and twinkling in his eyes. "You better go say hi to Tawny before you leave or she'll be upset."

"I will. Hey, how's Scott doing?"

"He's doing great. He just got promoted from running that store at the aquarium, and now he's the regional director—oversees all the stores from DC up to New York."

"That's great! Tell him I said hi, will you?" She gave Leon another big hug then grabbed Alec's arm and pulled him through the doorway and into the club area. The music was loud, but the crowd wasn't especially heavy so it was easy to move around the floor. AJ stood on her toes and looked around, then led Alec around the stage and toward the back corner, refusing to look back at him. Considering how bad he was dragging his feet and trying to pull her in the opposite direction, she could only imagine what would happen if she stopped to face him.

She waved to a few of the dancers on the floor that she recognized, but kept making her way to the corner. Alec finally escaped her hold on him and grabbed her hand, yanking her to a stop and turning her around, stepping close so he could lean over and talk to her. She at least gave him credit for keeping a blank look on his face. Either that, or he was still in a state of shock and didn't know what to think.

"Who is Scott?"

"What?" Of all the questions she had been expecting, that wasn't one of them. She bit the inside of her cheek to keep from laughing, and leaned forward to talk in his ear. "Scott is Leon's boyfriend. They've been together for something like ten years."

Alec swung his head around, looking back toward the door. "No way. Really? Hunh." He turned back, his hand tightening on her arm when she went to move away. "Oh no. No you don't. Not until you tell me...I mean, how do you know...did you use to...?"

That was one of the questions she had been expecting. At least, part of one of the questions, since Alec seemed to have trouble finishing the sentence. Part of her was sorely tempted to play it up, to tell him yes, she had been a dancer and that yes, she used to work here, just to see what his reaction would be. But he seemed so shell-shocked as it was that she didn't want to take a chance and send him over the edge.

"No Alec, I've never worked here. I did a freelance piece on some of the girls last year." She gently pried her arm free of his loose hold and turned away, not sure what to make of the relieved expression that crossed his face. He caught up to her and took the lead just as they approached the alcove where half a dozen of his teammates were gathered. Some of the players—those who didn't have their eyes glued to the stage—greeted Alec, then stared in surprise when they noticed her standing just behind him.

AJ pursed her lips and looked around in feigned innocence, waiting to see how Alec would handle her introduction and explain her appearance here. He still looked as shocked as he had when they first arrived—even more so. And she still couldn't figure out why he thought bringing her here had been a good idea. Although, judging from his reaction in the parking lot, he really *hadn't* realized exactly where he was bringing her. And if it had been any other club, she would have never stepped foot inside.

The lack of conversation finally caught her attention, and she turned to find several sets of eyes focused on her. The looks ranged from speculative to wary to intrigued. She smiled at the two players she actually knew—Ian Donovan and Randy Michaels— but the others were barely more than familiar faces. Yeah, she knew who they were, but she hadn't really had any interaction with them.

"You seriously brought your girlfriend here?" Jean-Pierre Larocque asked in his slight French-Canadian accent. He tipped a beer bottle back and drank deeply as his gaze roamed over her with an appreciative gleam. He was slouched down on the bench seat, his lean legs stretched out before him, a dark red polo pulled tight across his broad chest.

AJ crossed her arms and stared back with an unimpressed look on her face. Jean-Pierre was another one of the hockey team's attractive players, but he was too cocky. He offered her a half-smile then turned to Alec. "That is so wrong, Kolchak. No wonder you never go anywhere with us."

"She's not my girlfriend, Larocque. And stop staring, it's

disrespectful." This time it was AJ's turn to swing a surprised gaze in Alec's direction. He was actually telling someone to stop staring? When had he ever noticed before? He wouldn't meet her gaze. In fact, his gaze wasn't resting in any one spot, just shot from place to place every few seconds.

Everywhere except on her. And the stage.

She almost started laughing when she realized it. Alec was embarrassed! Embarrassed from either being in a strip club or from bringing her to a strip club. Or both. Probably both. She was getting ready to say something when she heard a squeal and felt thin arms wrap around her from behind.

"Amber, sweetie! Leon said you were here."

AJ turned, smiling as Tawny jumped up and down, her ample bare breasts barely jiggling with the movement. Tawny squealed again and gave her another big hug then stepped back, clasped AJ's face in both hands, and planted a loud kiss on her lips.

Stunned silence echoed from the seven men behind her. A split second later AJ heard a bottle fall to the floor with a muted splash, and she turned to see seven sets of eyes glued on the two of them. She looked down at Jean-Pierre, at the now empty hand he still held in front of him, seemingly oblivious to the fact that he just dropped his beer.

AJ and Tawny shared a knowing look and rolled their eyes simultaneously. Jean-Pierre blinked at them, shifted in his seat, then looked at Alec, who was still staring in mute shock.

"Since she's not your girlfriend, I'll take her."

The words triggered something in Alec and he snapped out of his daze. "Go to hell Larocque. AJ, we're leaving." He grabbed her hand and tugged, pulling her away from Tawny, away from his teammates. She dug her heels in to stop him but it was no good. AJ looked over her shoulder and saw Tawny waving good-bye, a twinkle in her eye as she made a 'call me' motion then turned her attention to the cocky French-Canadian.

AJ said good-bye to Leon in much the same way as Alec rushed her out of the club and to his car. He opened the door for her, giving her barely enough time to get situated before closing it and climbing in on the other side. She turned to look at him, surprised to see his jaw clenched and his brows lowered in a scowl. His hands were fisted around the steering wheel as he pulled out of the parking lot, and he refused to look at her.

"Alec—"

"AJ, please." He turned to glance at her, and she was taken aback at the steely look in his eyes. "Don't say anything. Not a word. Please. Just...don't say anything."

AJ clamped her mouth shut and faced straight ahead, wondering what it was she had done to upset him this time.

#

Alec unlocked the door to the condo and opened it as AJ pushed past him, not even looking at him. He gritted his teeth at the physical contact but said nothing, just closed the door behind him and tossed his keys on the hall table before following her into the living room.

She kept going, turning through the formal dining room into the kitchen. He heard the refrigerator open and close, then her footsteps as she retraced her path into the living room, a large can of iced tea in her hand. She carefully stepped around him, not touching him, not even looking at him.

"AJ—"

"Good night, Alec." She kept going, heading for the stairs, her foot touching the first one before Alec moved after her, grabbing her arm to stop her from walking away. She turned and finally looked at him, an expression of impatience written clearly on her face. Impatience, and something that looked like disappointment. Alec dropped her arm but didn't move away, just looked down at her, trying to figure out what to say.

The night had not gone even remotely close to how he had expected, not that he had known what to expect. All he wanted was for them to go out and have fun and get over the awkward distance that had developed between them the last couple of days. To get back to the light bantering relationship they had.

Yeah, and taking her to a strip club was the perfect choice. Christ, he still couldn't believe he had done that. He hadn't been thinking, hadn't even realized that it was a strip club at first because he had been so distracted just by having her sitting next to him.

But she had taken it in stride and even surprised him by going in. It didn't matter that she had obviously been there before, and that she knew people there. Although yeah, that had surprised him even more, but not for long.

But even after that shock, he had stupidly thought there was still a chance for them to just kind of hang out and have fun.

Until that asshole Jean-Pierre Larocque—who Alec actually used to like before tonight—had opened his mouth. Irritation had swiftly taken over Alec when he had caught Jean-Pierre blatantly ogling AJ. He had been ready to leave right then and there.

And then the stripper had come over and rubbed against AJ, had actually kissed her and...shit, there was no doubt in Alec's mind that every single one of his teammates had an instant hard-on at the sight. And *that* infuriated him, knowing exactly what was going through their minds as they stared at AJ. They had absolutely no right to stare at her like that, to think what they were thinking about her.

And he knew exactly what they were thinking, because the same thoughts had raced through his mind. Which was bad enough because—

"Alec! Do you want something or are you just going to stand there giving me dirty looks all night?"

He shook his head and realized he had been staring at AJ, though he didn't think he was giving her dirty looks. What was it she asked? Did he want something? If she only knew...

He stepped forward and grabbed her, pulling her toward him and dropping his mouth to hers so fast that she stumbled against him. It took less than a second for him to realize that the move was one of the stupidest he had ever made, and he stepped back, aided by AJ pushing against his chest with her free hand.

"Shit, shit. I'm sorry. God, that was so stupid." Alec ran his hands through his hair and down across his face, almost afraid to look at AJ. She was staring at him with one eyebrow raised, a look of disbelief etched across her features.

"Yeah, I get it. Typical male reaction. See two girls together and *boing*! Whatever. Good night Kolchak."

"Wait!" He reached for her again before she could turn around, but wisely stopped before touching her. "Is that what you think this is about? A quick fuck because of what happened back there? Christ, AJ. Is that what you really think of me?"

"So, what are you saying? You and your buddies didn't get turned on back there? It didn't effect you at all?"

"No! Trust me, I know exactly what was going through everyone's minds and it pisses me off. And I'd be lying if I said it didn't have a certain...effect...on me, which pisses me off even more. But that's not what this is about, AJ."

"Really? Then what is this about?" She crossed her arms in front of her, the can of tea dangling from one hand, and leaned one shoulder against the wall. It was the perfect picture of casual disbelief and impatience and Alec gritted his teeth, trying to figure out what he wanted to say.

"It's...I..."

"Because you know, Alec, you've pretty much gone out of your way to ignore me since the other night, and you made it quite obvious that you think it was a huge mistake so I'm not sure what you think—"

"What! I have not been ignoring—"

"Good night Alec." AJ turned and began the climb up the stairs, leaving Alec standing there staring after her. He gritted his teeth as he caught himself staring at her tight ass, hugged in the soft denim of her jeans. It took him all of five seconds to take off up the stairs after her and jump in front of her before she could open the door to the guest bedroom.

"I didn't mean to ignore you. I was, but I didn't mean to. I didn't know what to say to you or how to act and then you stopped talking to me and then I was afraid that anything I did say would only make things worse, only it turns out that it made it worse anyway."

AJ frowned at him but didn't try to push past him into her room, which he figured was a good sign until she rolled her eyes at him. "I have no idea what you just said."

Alec took a deep breath and ran his hands through his hair again, trying to swallow his frustration. It was no surprise she didn't understand, not when he didn't quite know what he was trying to say himself. "I don't know what I'm trying to say, either. It's just...I like how we always joked around and now that's all changed and I wish it hadn't. Except every time I look at you, all I want to do is...never mind. Forget it."

"No, tell me. What?" AJ looked up at him, her eyes curious, and he wondered if she really didn't know. How could she not know? He shook his head and let out a deep breath, figuring what the hell. It wasn't like he could make things any worse than they already were.

He lifted his hand and cupped his palm against her cheek, encouraged when she didn't immediately pull away. So he took a chance and cupped his second hand against her face and stepped closer, running his thumb along her lower lip. Tension immediately gripped him, and he had to clear his throat before he could speak.

"All I have wanted to do since you walked out of my room the other morning is chase after you and pull you back into bed." He still couldn't read the expression in her eyes so he leaned forward and gently touched his lips to hers. He increased the pressure, just a little, and inwardly rejoiced when she didn't pull away. Her hand reached up and closed around his bicep, squeezing, but she didn't push him away.

He deepened the kiss, coaxing her mouth to open under his, exploring her mouth with his tongue, feeling her hand glide up his arm and across his shoulder, then slide down across his chest. She fisted her hand in his shirt and gently pulled away, resting her forehead against his shoulder, her breaths coming in short gasps that matched his own.

"And this has nothing to do with the strip club?" Her voice was a hesitant whisper, and it took more control than Alec would have thought not to laugh at her uncertainty. He reached up for her hand and cradled it in his, then dragged it down his front, not stopping until her palm was cupping his hard-on. His breath hissed as she pressed her hand against him, rubbing, squeezing.

"I have been walking around with this for the last two days, non-stop, so no, this has nothing to do with tonight."

AJ's eyes were wide and uncertain as she stared up at him. Their blue depths swirled with a mix of hesitancy and desire, and Alec realized he should have done this two days ago, instead of letting her walk out of his room, out of his bed.

He grabbed the can from her hand and tossed it to the floor, then guided both of her hands up around his neck. Alec grabbed her around the waist and lifted her, biting back a groan as she wrapped her legs around his hips. Each step he took toward his room was exquisite agony as she rubbed against him, their eyes still locked together. He braced her against his bedroom door, and tried to reach around her to turn the knob.

AJ tilted her hips against his and he forgot about opening the door, just crushed his mouth against hers and wedged her between his body and the door. Her hands roamed over him, pulling at his shirt, yanking it up between them. His breath hitched as her hands raked against his bare chest, and he pulled at her own shirt, needing to feel her flushed skin against his.

AJ broke the kiss, leaning her head back against the door as he ran his lips along her neck and along her collarbone. "Alec...Alec, we need to talk..."

"No. No talking." He claimed her mouth again and turned the door knob, tightening his hold on her as the door swung open. He reached the bed in record time and gently lowered AJ to the mattress, following her down, her legs still wrapped tightly around him.

Alec pushed up, breaking away from her just long enough to pull his shirt over his head, then leaned down and removed hers as well. His gaze roamed over her body, at the fullness of her breasts spilling over the lacy edges of her sheer yellow bra, at the smooth expanse of her flat belly. He trailed his hands along her skin, starting at her wrists and working his way up her arms, across her shoulders and down along her chest. He teased the taut peaks of her nipples with his thumb, then leaned over her, taking one nipple in his mouth, teasing it through the lace of her bra, groaning when she arched up into him, her hands digging into his shoulders.

He pulled back, his hands still trailing downward until he reached the waistband of her jeans. With a quick motion, he unfastened them and skimmed them down over her hips and thighs, following his hands with his lips, dragging his mouth across the skimpy triangle of her matching lacy thong. Again AJ arched against him, her hands curling at her sides, clenching the comforter.

He teased her clit through the lace, sliding his hand under her to cup her bottom, to hold her more tightly against his mouth. Her body arched into him as a soft moan escaped her, feeding his own excitement.

Alec pulled away from her, dragging his mouth down the inside of her thigh, as he pulled her boots from her feet then dragged her jeans all the way off. He reached for the boots and put them back on her feet before dragging his mouth back up her legs, across the lacy thong, up her flat stomach until he was poised above her, bracing his weight on his arms as he looked down at her.

"Do you have any idea how much those boots turn me on?"

Her eyes fluttered open at his hoarse confession and slowly focused on him. Alec wasn't sure what she saw in his gaze, but her lips turned up in a slight smile, a gleam in her eye.

"Hm, they do?" She ran her hands up his arms to his chest, wrapping her legs around him once more, pulling him closer against her before she tightened her hold and tried to roll. Alec grabbed her as he spun around, pulling her on top, feeling her settle against him as she pushed herself up, straddling him.

He reached out and grabbed her hips, holding her steady as she ground against him, her head tilted back, her bottom lip held between her teeth. Alec grew even harder as she rubbed against him, straining against the confining denim that kept him from burying himself deep inside her hot sweetness.

He let go of her hips to unfasten his jeans, pulling the zipper down and reaching in to free himself. AJ slid down his legs, leaning forward and grabbing the waist band of his jeans and tugging them down, allowing him to free himself even more. Her hand tightened over his, keeping it in place, then began stroking, up and down, long excruciating moves along his hard shaft.

Alec clenched his jaw, his breath hissing between his teeth when AJ leaned forward and ran her tongue over him, up his stomach and chest, the soft tendrils of her hair teasing his bare flesh, her hand still guiding his in long strokes, faster, harder.

"I want you now, AJ."

She stretched against him, nipping at his chest before looking up at him, the heat in her eyes searing. "Then take me." She pushed herself up, straddling him again, rubbing against him even as he stretched across the bed, reaching for the nightstand, cursing under his breath until his fingers closed over the packet of condoms. He grabbed one and brought it to his mouth, tearing open the foil with his teeth.

AJ rocked herself against him, liquid heat forging hot iron, and Alec damn near forgot about the condom, came close to reaching for her, to sliding her lacy thong out of the way and shoving his cock deep inside her. He sucked in his breath, wanting to do nothing more than just that.

He reached between them and sheathed himself with the condom then slid his fingers along the edge of her thong, easing the damp material to the side, teasing her clit first with his thumb, then with the tip of his cock.

AJ sucked in a deep breath, her head falling back as he continued to tease her, her hips surging forward, seeking him. Alec had thought to tease her, to drive her wild, and had succeeded in doing the same thing to himself. No longer wanting to hold back, no longer wanting to tease, he grabbed her hips and lifted her above him, whispering her name until she opened her eyes and looked down at him. He held her gaze, his hands tightening around her hips, guiding her onto him, driving himself into her with a quick thrust that took his breath away.

Their bodies stilled, their gazes locked, then Alec began moving, pumping his hips, driving himself deep inside her, pulling out, driving again. AJ's eyes drifted shut and her head fell back, her breasts thrust forward, the hard peaks of her tightened nipples pushing at the lace of her bra. He reached up and tugged at the material, pulling downward until her breast spilled out, filling his hands. He massaged her, pulling at her nipples, tweaking the hard points with his fingers as he continued to drive into her.

AJ's breathing became harsher, small gasps as her hips met his, rocking against him, thrusting, harder, faster. She leaned further back, resting her hands low on his thighs, twisting the denim of his jeans in her fists as she matched his rhythm.

Alec felt her muscles tighten around him, felt the first spasm rock through her. She moaned, his name a whisper on her lips as her body closed around him. Alec grabbed her hips, holding her down against him, and drove into her harder, once, twice, and felt her shatter around him, her muscles tightening around him, squeezing him, milking him. He threw his head back, lost in the feel of her wet heat quivering around him, then thrust deeper inside her, his own explosion rocking through him, tearing her name from his lips in a guttural moan.

ELEVEN

Alec stood next to the bed, gazing down at AJ's sleeping form. She was curled in the middle of the bed, clinging to the pillow where he had been sleeping just a short while ago. Her tousled hair was fanned around her face. The comforter had fallen from her shoulders, exposing the curve of her bare arm and breast, the soft rise and fall of her chest.

His groin tightened just at the sight of her sleeping so peacefully in his bed. He was tempted, so tempted, to climb back in with her, to wake her with soft kisses, to sink into her sleepy warmth and feel her come awake, alive, around him.

Just as he had done barely more than an hour ago, for the third time that night.

They had slept, tangled together, for a short time after their first frantic encounter. The second time had been just as wild, as if they couldn't get enough of each other.

The last time...Alec breathed in deeply, the images still burning in his memory. AJ had been curled against him, her head tucked into his shoulder, her hand curled against his chest. He had run his hands over her warm skin, rained gentle kisses along her jaw and lips until she reached for him, welcoming him into her sleepy body.

And he had made love to her, slowly, gently, drawing out their pleasure until it became exquisite torture, until they found release together. Sweet, warm release. As sweet as the feel of AJ curled against him, her body warm and soft and trusting in sleep.

Alec took another deep breath then leaned over the bed, gently pulling the comforter up around her shoulders and placing a kiss on her temple. AJ stirred slightly, moving toward him, then settled deeper into the mattress with a soft sigh. He smiled then backed away toward the door, his eyes memorizing the sight of her in his bed.

Alec grabbed his overnight bag from the floor and walked out of the room, closing the door behind him with a quiet click, already looking forward to returning home after tomorrow afternoon's game.

#

AJ came awake slowly, cocooned in the warmth of the fluffy comforter. She stretched, a lazy lengthening of her body as she rolled from her side to her back. The room had a gray cast to the light, giving the impression of early morning, but when she turned her head to look out the balcony doors, she could see it was raining, the sky dark and overcast.

She stretched again and looked at her watch, surprised to see that it was nearly noon. Knowing she should get up, she closed her eyes instead, wanting nothing more than to return to sleep.

Alec was gone. She had known that even before coming fully awake. But she had a hazy memory—or maybe it was just wishful thinking—of him leaning over her and kissing her good bye, mere hours after he had so slowly, so expertly, so carefully made love to her.

That last time had been her undoing. She knew it as certainly as she knew her own name. It had been easier to hold herself back, to keep a piece of herself safe, when the sexual encounters had been wild, frantic...

Who was she kidding? She had been in trouble long before the sex had even entered the picture. Alec's tender love making had only pushed her over the edge enough for her to admit that...well, that she had been pushed over the edge.

It was the last thing she should have allowed to happen. Absolutely no good could come from it. None.

She curled onto her side and reached for Alec's pillow, scooping it closer to her, holding it against her much as she had held him in her sleep. His scent still clung to it, a faint woodsy smell mingled with the slightest spicy hint. AJ closed her eyes and nestled deeper into the mattress, allowing herself the luxury of replaying snippets of the night before in her mind. She would give herself another hour before getting up and getting dressed, another hour to pretend before going back into the guest room and pulling out her laptop to write.

Another hour to talk herself out of the five-hour drive to Pittsburgh to talk to him.

Another hour before gathering her things together, to prepare for when Alec returned home after the away game.

Because there was no doubt in her mind that things would change again after he saw the article tomorrow. And he *would* see it. Either before or after the game, he would see it, and things would never be the same.

#

Alec batted away the practice pucks being hit his way, warming up before the game. He had a good feeling about tonight, about the way the team was gelling together even better than usual. Games against Pittsburgh were always high energy, fueled by the fans' enthusiasm and even by their taunting barbs. It was an age-old classic rivalry, not quite taken in stride by the players from both sides. And it wasn't unusual to have an excessive amount of fights when the two teams met, regardless of whose home ice the game was being played on.

The energy from the fans was already filling the arena, feeding the players' own energy levels. Alec fended off the last few practice shots then pushed his helmet up and grabbed the water bottle off the back of the net. He took a long swig then pushed away from the net, skating toward the players' bench.

Alec had just walked into the box and was heading for the hallway when he heard his name called. He turned to see one of the opposing players leaning across the boards, a sly smile on his face.

"Are you sure you're up to playing tonight, Kolchak?"

Alec took a step closer, his brows raised in question as another player skated up to the bench. "Against you guys? Bring it on."

The two laughed and nudged each other, smirking. "Well, considering how warm and sensitive you are, we thought you might sit tonight out. We wouldn't want to be hurting your feelings."

They laughed again and skated away, leaving Alec staring after them in confusion. Ian Donovan pushed against the door and entered the player's bench, calling a few rude comments to the retreating duo.

"What the hell was that all about?" Alec asked him as they walked back toward the visiting team's locker room. Ian shook his head and kept walking.

"Nothing. Don't worry about it." Ian wouldn't look at him, so Alec grabbed his arm and pulled him to a stop.

"Out with it, Donovan. What's up?" Ian sighed and stepped away, suddenly looking everywhere but at Alec, who stepped even closer to him, a threatening look on his face. "What the hell is going on?"

"Guess you haven't seen today's paper."

"Paper?" A feeling of dread threatened to drop over Alec but he shoved it away. "What paper?"

"The newspaper."

The dread came back, and he was unable to push it away this time. Alec swallowed and tightened his hold on his stick, gripping it so hard he was surprised the graphite didn't shatter in his glove. He clenched his jaw, breathing in deeply, then let the breath out in a rush, staring at Ian with cool eyes.

"I want to see it."

"Alec, really, it's not bad—"

"Now."

Ian sighed and turned away, motioning for Alec to follow. He swallowed again and loosened his grip on the stick then took off after Ian, dread increasing with each step.

#

The house was quiet, eerily so. She hadn't bothered with any lights either upstairs or down, preferring to sit in the dark, with only the reflected harbor lights keeping her company.

AJ sat in the corner of the leather sofa, dressed in a loose pair of sweat pants and one of Alec's t-shirts. Her legs were curled under her, and she stared across the room out the open French doors. Her gaze was locked on the blue neon waves that ringed the aquarium's dolphin pavilion across the harbor, and her mind randomly wandered from thought to thought.

She glanced at her watch then leaned her head against the back of the sofa, holding the throw pillow in her arms, wondering how much longer before Alec got home.

That was going to be an encounter she wasn't looking forward to, especially after seeing that afternoon's game. Any slim hope she might have held that he hadn't seen the article shattered before the first period was even half-way over. By the time the full-out brawl broke out at the start of the third period, AJ wanted to do nothing more than get in her car and drive as fast as possible for as far as she could.

But that would have been running away, and it struck her as being entirely too cowardly.

An hour later, the thought crossed her mind that being a coward might have been the smartest choice when she heard the door click open in the foyer...and slam shut loud enough to make her jump.

AJ closed her eyes and told herself to stay still, to remain quiet. Nothing she said now would help anything. She repeated that to herself several times as Alec's footsteps came closer. He stopped several feet away, and she heard the heavy thud of his bag hitting the floor, followed by the sharp clatter of his keys as they hit the table hard enough to let her know that he did more than just casually toss them.

The silence that had been almost peaceful earlier in the day was now heavy and oppressive, suffocating. AJ opened her eyes and turned her head just the tiniest bit, just enough to catch a glimpse of Alec behind her, standing off to the side. And even though there wasn't any light, she could see him staring down at her. That small look was enough to let her know that any chance of his ire being reduced during the long drive back from the game had never materialized.

The silence stretched out, painful in its intensity, yet Alec still didn't move. She could feel him standing off to the side behind her, could feel his eyes focused on her, could feel the tension and anger radiating off of him. She shifted, turning on the sofa so she could get a better look at him, feeling vulnerable with him standing behind her the way he was.

"Did you watch the game?" His voice was quiet, almost harsh, his eyes intense as he looked down at her.

AJ pulled the pillow closer to her, like a shield, and nodded. "Yeah."

"Yeah." Alec looked away from her, his hands fisted on his hips. Even with such little light, she could see the flare in his eyes, the muscle twitching in his clenched jaw. He shifted his weight from one foot to the other, glanced down at her, looked away again. "And...nothing to say?"

The question surprised AJ, her mouth opening silently then closing. She had no idea how to respond, no idea what Alec expected her to say. The game had disintegrated rapidly, not completely surprising considering the long-running rivalry between the two teams. But even she had been able to tell, just from watching on the television, that there had been something more going on. She didn't know what, and wasn't entirely sure she could guess—or that she wanted to.

Then there had been the on-ice brawl...the one that had included both goalies. Yeah, it happened. Maybe once a decade. Alec had drawn two major penalties and a game misconduct, and been ejected from the game—a personal record for him.

The damage, of course, had been done before all that even happened, with the Banners losing 10-2. Alec had asked if she had anything to say. What was she supposed to say? Did he expect her to apologize? Was he saying the whole afternoon's debacle was her fault?

AJ shifted again on the sofa, uncurling her legs from beneath her and pulling them against her chest instead. She still held onto the pillow, feeling better with it in her hands, absently picking at the corner trim and shaking her head before answering. "I'm not sure what you expect me to say."

Alec let out a deep breath then suddenly turned and walked toward the kitchen, the soles of his dress shoes clicking loudly against the hardwood floor. Light from the kitchen filtered into the living room, chasing away the corner shadows and making AJ feel somehow more vulnerable. Part of her was tempted to get up and follow him into the kitchen, another part was still tempted to just get up and run.

She did neither, just waited until she heard the refrigerator door slam close, waited until Alec walked out of the kitchen, pausing in the doorway of the dining room. He leaned his shoulder against the doorframe and took a long drink from the beer bottle in his hand before staring at her.

AJ finally looked at him then sucked in her own breath and winced when she saw the marks on his face. There was a cut under his left eye, with a dark bruise under that on his cheekbone. His lip was slightly swollen, and she thought she could see a cut at the corner of his mouth as well. She almost jumped from the sofa and ran over to him, to see if he was okay, to tend his injuries, but something in the way he was standing there stopped her. Suppressed energy and tension radiated from him, filling the entire room, holding her in place.

"Does it hurt?" It was barely more than a whisper. Alec remained quiet for so long she didn't think he heard her, and she was ready to repeat the question when he pushed away from the doorway, his stride long and angry, his footsteps heavy as he walked into the living room.

"More than I would have thought." Anger vibrated in his voice as he passed her without a single look on his way to the stairs. AJ flinched when she heard his bedroom door slam shut a minute later, and she couldn't help but think that he hadn't been talking about his injuries.

TWELVE

Sharp banging echoed somewhere nearby, startling AJ out of her restless sleep. She pushed up on her elbow and brushed the hair out of her eyes, squinting against the light streaming in through the open doors. The muscles in her neck protested when she looked around, trying to clear her mind of the last remnants of sleep. She untangled her legs from the blanket and slowly sat all the way up with a groan as her stiff muscles protested sleeping on the sofa all night.

AJ frowned. She didn't remember falling asleep here; she must have dozed off after Alec stormed upstairs last night. So where had the blanket come from?

Sounds of movement and more banging came from the kitchen. Alec was obviously awake already and fixing something to eat. He must have been the one to cover her with the blanket sometime during the night. AJ thought she should probably go into the kitchen and thank him, but she couldn't bring herself to do more than prop her elbows on her knees and lower her head into her hands.

"There's coffee if you want some." Alec spoke from the doorway, and AJ briefly wondered how he had known she was awake. It didn't matter. What mattered was that his voice sounded even more distant and chilled than it did last night.

She bit back a sigh and pushed herself off the sofa then shuffled to the large gourmet kitchen. It didn't matter that one leg of her sweatpants had pushed up to her knee, or that Alec's shirt was twisted around her waist. She focused only on making it to the coffee pot, on pouring the dark brew into a large mug and taking a deep sip. It burned as it slipped past her tongue, the heat hitting her system before the caffeine. She took another sip then cautiously searched out Alec above the rim.

He was standing by the stove, throwing things into a frying pan, his back to her. There was no doubt he was still mad, not if his clipped motions were any indication. She took a few more sips of the coffee, topped off the mug, then walked over to the center island and pulled out a stool. A newspaper tossed on the counter caught her attention, and she paused before finally taking a seat, her eyes on the bold headline above her byline.

Under that was a full color picture of Alec in the net, his helmet tipped back, his mouth slightly open as he drank from a water bottle. The picture was a great one, capturing the angles of his face, the depth of his eyes. AJ figured that a large portion of Baltimore's female population were now members of the Alec Kolchak fan club. Not that she had any room to talk, since she qualified as club President.

She shifted on the stool to get comfortable, hooking her feet around the legs and reaching out to pull the paper closer. She had read it yesterday, of course, but there was still a small flutter of excitement at seeing it in full color, at the sight of her byline, so prominent and—

Suddenly pulled from her hands and tossed to the counter by the sink. AJ tucked her chin down and took another sip, not daring to look at Alec. He hadn't said anything since letting her know about the coffee. After ripping the paper out of her hands like he just did, he didn't *have* to say anything for her to know he was still upset.

So AJ sat there, sipping her coffee and swinging her foot back and forth, staring at the island countertop as Alec finished cooking. His back was still to her, so she watched as he pulled the pan off the stove and tilted it over a plate.

Her stomach suddenly grumbled, loud enough that there was no way Alec could have missed hearing it. She ducked her head and pretended to be focused only on drinking her coffee, then jumped in surprise when a plate and silverware were pushed in front of her.

"Eat."

AJ looked up, but he had already turned around, giving her his back once more. Which, she guessed, was fair enough, since he had gone back to mixing more things in the frying pan. She sighed and reached for the fork, taking a small bite of the omelet and trying not to groan in satisfaction at the taste.

"This is good, thank you."

Her words hung in the air, eliciting zero response from Alec. She took another bite and chewed, staring at his back, willing him to turn around and look at her. Several minutes passed until he tipped the pan over a second plate and slid his own omelet out, then tossed the pan into the sink with a bang. He grabbed his own fork then finally turned around, leaning against the counter to eat, his legs casually crossed, not even looking at her.

But he didn't have to look at her in order for her to see the cuts and bruises on his face. They looked worse than they did last night, and she didn't know if it was because of the time that had passed, or if it was because she could see them in the light now.

She inwardly winced as Alec took another bite of his breakfast, watching as he made sure to stay away from the cut on the side of his lip. How he was eating at all without writhing in agony was beyond her. It hurt just to look at; she couldn't imagine how it actually felt.

"I can do without being stared at while I'm eating."

AJ started then looked back down at her own breakfast, feeling guilty at being caught staring. Then she just felt irritated. She finished her omelet and pushed the plate away, then took a few more sips of coffee before looking up at Alec.

He was still leaning against the counter, his legs still crossed, still eating. Still ignoring her.

"Okay, I get that you're pissed off. Are we going to talk about it or not?"

He looked up at her, his eyes dark, a spark of irritation flaring in their depths before he looked away again. AJ let out a sigh, deliberately loud and impatient, just to see what he would do. Again, he gave her another dark look before turning away, placing the empty plate in the sink.

"What? Didn't feel like throwing that in like you did the frying pan?" AJ wished she could take the words back as soon as they left her mouth. They were sarcastic and immature. It didn't matter that they relieved some of her own frustration. At least, it was obvious it didn't matter to Alec. He again turned his dark gaze on her and just stared at her, a muscle twitching in his clenched jaw.

A few long, quiet seconds stretched between them before he stepped to the island counter and reached for her plate. His eyes still locked on hers, he stepped back and threw it into the sink, where it landed with a shattering crash as it hit the other plate and frying pan. "Like that?"

AJ bit the inside of her cheek to keep from smiling. This was *not* funny. It really wasn't. Alec was more than just a little upset. Anger and frustration rolled off him as he watched her, the emotions flaring in his eyes. And AJ felt her own anger spark to life under his gaze, an irrational ignition of emotion that had been left to simmer for too long. She leaned back on the stool and crossed her arms, fixing him with her own cool stare.

"So are we going to have this out or not? Because, like I said, it's obvious you're pissed. Are you going to tell me why?"

"Am I going to tell you why?" Alec repeated, his voice dangerously low and quiet. He reached behind him and grabbed the paper from the counter, then flung it to the island countertop. "Christ AJ, why do you think? Do you think maybe this could have something to do with it?"

AJ glanced down at the paper then back at Alec, understanding he was upset about the feature, but not really understanding why. A blade of defensiveness knifed through her, and she sat up straighter. "Do you want to tell me what is so wrong with this?"

"What's wrong with it? What do you think is wrong with it? This isn't a simple story! It's more like a damned expose in a fucking tabloid."

AJ jumped back so quickly she almost fell off the stool. A hard slap would have hurt less than the words he had just thrown at her. Her heart hammered deep in her chest, pounding below her rib cage and against her lungs, making her breaths come sharp and quick. She returned Alec's stare, making no attempt to hide her anger and her hurt. Something flashed in the depths of his eyes and he looked away, taking a deep breath and running his hands through his hair.

"I didn't mean it like that."

"The hell you didn't." AJ lowered herself from the stool, standing ramrod straight as she faced Alec, her chin held high in stubborn defiance.

"AJ...this isn't what I agreed to. This," he grabbed the paper and held it clenched in one fist between them, "this isn't an interview."

"You're right, it's not. It's a feature article. And it's a damned good one."

"It's not what I agreed to! You've made me out to be some kind of...of...I don't know. Some kind of elite pretty boy."

"What are you talking about? That is absolutely ridiculous."

"Is it?"

"Yeah, it is. The feature doesn't turn you into anything—it just brings out a human side to all the boring stats that you've hid behind all the years you've been playing."

"Well I hate to break it to you, sweetheart, but the general consensus now is that I'm a pretty boy. I believe the term 'henpecked pansy ass' was also used."

AJ closed her mouth with an audible snap. Had she really heard him correctly? The dark look was still on his face, the flare of anger and frustration still lingered in his eyes. Yes, she had heard him correctly. She swallowed and took a deep breath, letting it out slowly as realization dawned on her.

"Is that what all the fighting was about last night?" The muscle ticked in his jaw again, giving her the answer. "Really? So where did the 'henpecked' come from? Because I don't get that one—"

"Dammit AJ, this isn't funny!" His shout echoed in the silence of the kitchen, ringing off the stainless steel appliances and granite floor and countertops to bounce back at both of them. Alec met her stare and their eyes locked for several minutes until, finally, his lips twitched upwards. It was the smallest twitch, but it was there. His lips twitched again and he quickly turned away, wrapping his hands around his neck and leaning his head back with a frustrated groan.

"It's really not funny," he said again. Except this time his voice was muffled and hoarse, almost like he was choking. AJ pulled herself back onto the stool and propped her elbows on the island top as she watched him.

"So...are you, like, laughing? Or are you choking? Because if you're choking I'm not sure I want to help you."

"I'm not choking." Alec stood with his back to her for

another minute then finally turned to face her with a heavy sigh. She watched him warily as he looked at her, almost as if he was studying her, before he took a step forward and leaned his arms against the island. The move put him dangerously close and she sat back just a little, unable to gauge this new mood and needing to put distance between them.

"I'm sorry about the 'tabloid' comment."

"Okay." AJ sat back even further, still cautious, not entirely trusting him. "I'm sorry about the 'henpecked' comment."

Alec stared at her, the marks on his face making him look even more menacing. "Why? You didn't make it."

"No, but I figured I may as well apologize since you're blaming me for it."

Alec hung his head and muttered to himself. AJ couldn't quite make out what he was saying, but she had a sudden suspicion that he was counting to himself. Except he kept counting long past the time he should have reached 'ten'.

Which she thought was kind of insulting.

He finally looked up at her, the darkness and frustration gone from his eyes. "I let the trash talk get to me last night. And I believe 'henpecked' came because everyone knows you wrote the article."

"Everyone who? In case you didn't notice, the byline says 'AJ Johnson'. Not *Amber Johnson*. There's a reason I use 'AJ', you know. People don't take people named 'Amber' seriously."

Alec looked a little taken aback. He actually pushed himself up on his elbows, putting distance between them, and looked at her. "Is that what you think?"

"No, it's what I know. Would you read a serious sports piece by someone named 'Amber'? No, you wouldn't."

"Well it doesn't matter what you think. Everyone knows who wrote it, no matter what name you used."

"That's because everyone on your team knows who I am."

"AJ, I'm not talking about the Banners. I'm talking about Pittsburgh."

She sat up straighter, trying not to smile. People knew who she was? That had to be a good thing. "Really? They knew who I was?"

"Yeah. The 'henpecked' came from them because I 'opened up' to a 'girl'."

Her brief excitement died at both Alec's look of amusement as well as his words. "What? Of all the...just wait until they're playing here. I can't believe—"

Alec's hand clamped over her mouth, stopping her tirade. Their eyes locked and her stomach did a little flip at the instant spark that shot between them. Alec quickly removed his hand and shifted back, pulling his gaze away.

"I just...why didn't you tell me about it, AJ? If you had told me, I wouldn't have been caught off-guard by the whole thing."

"I tried!"

"When?"

"Friday. As soon as I walked through the front door, I told you we needed to talk but you didn't want to hear it." He frowned as he thought back, and she could tell when he finally remembered by the spark of realization that flashed in his eyes. Alec stood up and walked around the edge of the island, coming closer to her. She scooted further back on the stool, wary, not quite sure what he was planning on doing. "And then, later that night, I said I wanted to talk but you—"

"Yeah, I remember." He stopped inches from her, towering over her, his eyes burning as he looked down at her.

"I really did try—" Alec didn't let her finish, just wrapped his arms around her and kissed her, claiming her mouth in a searing move of possession. She placed her hands against his chest, not pushing him away, but not giving him the leverage to get any closer, either. He gentled the kiss then broke away, pulling back only a few inches to stare at her.

She reached up and gently touched her fingertip first to the cut at the corner of his mouth then to the cut under his eye. He winced just the smallest bit but didn't pull away. "Does it hurt?"

"Would you kiss it and make it better if I said yes?" She thought he meant for the words to come out as a teasing joke, but his voice was a hoarse whisper instead. Heat simmered in his gaze, settled between them, smoldering. AJ leaned into his hold and tilted her head up, placing the lightest of kisses against the cut under his eye then moving lower, gently kissing the cut at the corner of his mouth.

His arms tightened around her and he pulled her closer, his mouth claiming hers in a kiss as light as hers had been. His touch was gentle, a feathery caress of his lips on hers. AJ curled her hands around his arms, feeling the hard muscle under her touch, the heat of his flesh through the thin cotton of his t-shirt. She ran her hands up his shoulders then down his back, her fingers tracing the sculpted ridges of his body.

Alec's kiss became bolder, possessive, his tongue seeking and finding hers as his hands moved along her body, down to her waist, her hips, her thighs. His touch ignited a trail of heat as his mouth continued its seduction of hers, unleashing any hesitation she had felt only minutes ago. She slid her hands lower down his back, into the waistband of his sweatpants, along the firm muscle of his ass.

Alec groaned and broke the kiss, his own hands reaching for the hem of her shirt and pulling it up, the palms of his hands skimming her flesh as he pushed the shirt up and pulled it over her head. "By the way, you look great in my shirt. But you look even better out of it," he whispered, his breath warm against her neck. AJ tilted her head back, her eyes closed, enjoying the sensation of his lips against her flesh, of the feel of his hands as they caressed and molded her breasts.

"You noticed, hm?"

"Hm-hm." Alec nuzzled her neck, his hands heavy and warm along her flesh, teasing. AJ swallowed against the sensation, wanting to lose herself in his touch, but needing to hold herself back. She slid her hands from his backside to his chest, finding the strength to grasp his wrists and pull his own hands away from her.

Alec lifted his head the smallest bit and stared down at her, confusion mingled with the heat in his dark eyes.

"I...does this mean you're not mad at me anymore?" AJ's voice sounded more like a desperate croak but she didn't bother to clear her throat and repeat her question, not when Alec smiled at her.

"No, I'm still a little mad. But I think this might go a long way to making me get over it." His own voice was as raspy as hers had been. He leaned forward, intent on kissing her again, but she pulled back, just a bit.

"Alec, I'm—"

"Shh. It doesn't matter."

"But I didn't mean—"

His mouth closed over hers, effectively quieting her. AJ surrendered to his touch, giving in to the quiet demands of both of their bodies. She clung to him as he grabbed her by the waist and lifted her, then gently sat her on the island countertop.

Where they both proceeded to make the other forget about anything but just the two of them.

THIRTEEN

If part one of the feature had turned Baltimore's female population into Alec Kolchak fans, the second part turned the city itself into hockey fans. Known more for its football team, baseball team, and local Natty Boh brew, Baltimore reserved a loyal—but small—fan base for its ice hockey team. If the increased crowds filling the stands for the last few games were an indication, that fan base was growing.

Alec pushed back his helmet and surveyed the crowd pushing against the boards of the practice rink. He couldn't remember the last time this many people had come out for one of their practices.

And if you asked him, that wasn't a good thing. It was great that game attendance was up, nobody argued that. The crowds at practice, however, were nothing but large distractions—just one more in a line of distractions he didn't need.

He turned to grab his water bottle just as Ian skated up to him, spraying him with a shower of ice. Alec filled his mouth with water, rinsed, then spit it out before taking a sip.

"Can you believe this?" Ian asked quietly, his eyes scanning the crowds. "I've never seen this many people at practice before."

"Yeah, I was just thinking the same thing. Coach is going to have to start closing them if this keeps up."

Ian continued scanning the crowd, slowly shaking his head. "I don't think they will. Why piss off the new fans, you know?" His searching eyes stopped and he nudged Alec. "Hey, isn't that AJ? What's she doing talking to them? And who's that guy with her?"

Alec turned in the direction Ian was pointing and frowned. AJ was supposed to be in a meeting with her editor. He looked closer and his frown grew deeper. The man with her *was* her editor. And they were talking to the team owner and two people he recognized as being from the PR and Marketing Department.

"Shit. That's her editor. This cannot be good." Alec and Ian continued watching the small group in silence, but there was no way Alec could tell what was happening. AJ finally looked over, an expression of dismay on her face. She offered him a small shrug, and mouthed something that made his stomach drop as he cursed.

"What? What did she say?"

Alec turned away from watching the group and slapped his stick against the ice then banged it against the pipe. "She said 'I'm sorry'. Shit, this is so not good."

"So what's going on?"

"I have no idea, but I have a bad feeling about it."

Ian watched him for a few seconds then tapped the blade of his stick against Alec's skate. "Well, she's your girlfriend, I suggest you do something about it."

"She's not my girlfriend." The denial flew from his mouth before he even realized he was going to say anything. An odd emotion crept over him, leaving him feeling hollow.

Ian snorted loudly, then shook his head. "Dude, not sure who you think you're fooling with that line but okay, if you say so."

Alec watched Ian skate away, then turned back to the stands to catch a glimpse of AJ. She was still in the middle of the small group but they were now walking away, and he quickly lost sight of her.

The odd hollow feeling stayed with him, though. AJ wasn't his girlfriend, so why did the denial leave him feeling empty? It wasn't as if they were dating, as if there was anything real between them.

Except for her laughter and smile. Except for the easy feeling of companionship and camaraderie that had grown between them. Except for the unexpected friendship he had found with her.

Except they went to sleep in each other's arms every night and they woke up curled together each morning.

Shit. So if she wasn't his girlfriend, what the hell was she? And what were they doing? He muttered to himself and grabbed the water bottle, squeezing a stream into his face and shaking it off as he repeated the question to himself.

What *were* they doing? And more importantly...what was it he wanted them to be doing?

#

Alec dimmed the dining room lights and took one last look at the set table, grinning to himself. As a surprise, he was sure AJ would enjoy it. The formal china and heavy silver utensils rested on fancy linen placemats—none of which he had ever bothered to use before—and the lit candles reflected off the heavy glass table and the crystal glassware. The real surprise was in the kitchen, keeping warm until she got home.

He glanced at his watch just as he heard the door open, and smiled again. Perfect timing, he thought, hitting the remote for the stereo system so soft music filled the room. He walked toward the living room just as AJ came through the foyer, her head down as she tossed her keys onto the table and sat her backpack on the floor.

He leaned against the door frame, just watching for a few seconds as she straightened and stretched, still not seeing him. She was wearing the outfit she had on earlier, a flowing sweater in a light brown and curve-hugging khaki pants. His gaze drifted down her legs and he smiled when he saw the pirate boots.

"Hey."

AJ turned, looking startled for a quick second when she saw him standing there. She offered him a smile that left too quickly but she stayed where she was. Alec frowned, noticing the tension around her mouth and the paleness of her skin.

He pushed himself away from the door frame and took several steps toward her. "Everything okay?"

"Yeah. I just...I've got a headache, that's all."

Alec closed the distance between them and pulled her into his arms, dropping a kiss on the top of her head as he gave her a hug, trying to ignore the effect she had on him. "Well, come in here. I have a surprise that might help."

She pulled out of his arms and offered him a brief smile that didn't quite meet her eyes, then let him lead her toward the dining room. She paused at the doorway, then looked up at him, giving him another small smile.

"Wow. Pretty fancy. What's the occasion?"

"No occasion." He led her to the table and pulled a chair out for her with a flourishing bow. AJ smiled again and took a seat, turning up to look at him, her bewilderment still clear on her face. He couldn't resist; he draped his arm along the back of the chair and leaned down, claiming her mouth in an all-too-brief kiss. "Wait here."

Alec walked into the kitchen and opened the oven, breathing in the warm scent of Italian spices as he pulled the tray out. Sitting it on the island, he turned and walked to the refrigerator and pulled out the bottle of wine. He had thought about opening one of the reds, but decided against it because of AJ's headache. He certainly didn't want to make it worse.

No, if things went well, he was hoping he'd be able to make her forget all about her headache.

He worked on uncorking the bottle and called into the dining room. "So how did your meeting go today?"

"Um...yeah, about that." The hesitancy in her voice caught his attention and he stepped into the dining room, the bottle of wine in his hand. AJ had her head propped in her hands, her hair falling around her face. She looked up briefly when he leaned over and poured wine into her glass, then muttered a quick thanks.

She didn't say anything else, so Alec went back into the kitchen and grabbed the tray from the island. He entered the dining room once more, the tray held out in front of him, and offered it to her with a small bow. AJ's light laughter drew a smile from him as he placed the tray in the middle of the table.

"Pizza! I knew something smelled good when I walked in."

"Nothing but the best." Alec took a seat across from her then slid a slice onto her offered plate before scooping one out for himself. "So about your meeting...?"

"Let's eat first." Her gaze dropped from his and she focused on eating the pizza, her bites small, almost hesitant. He could see the tension in her face, the small furrow in her creased brow as she did little more than nibble her food. She finally gave up and put the pizza down, then took a long sip of her wine.

"Are you sure you're feeling okay?"

She took another sip then pushed the glass away, giving him a slight nod. "Yeah. Listen, I just want you to know that I tried to stop it."

Alec paused with the pizza half-way to his mouth. The expression on her face was pure agony; he had thought it was from her headache, that she was getting another migraine, but maybe not. He put the pizza down and looked at her. "That sounds pretty ominous."

She met his eyes briefly then looked away and shrugged. "Not really. I mean, I don't think so. You might, though. Actually, the whole thing is really a bit funny and—"

"AJ, out with it."

"Um...they thought it would be interesting to get some shots of me on the ice. I don't know why, they just did, so I'll be practicing with you tomorrow." She finished in a rush then grabbed the wine glass and drained it.

Alec sat back in his chair at her news, torn between laughing and leaping across the glass table to kiss her. This is what had her looking so miserable and tense? Unless he was missing something, the news wasn't terrible. Had she really thought he would be upset by it?

"That's it?"

She finally looked up at him, her eyes still wary and hesitant. "You're not mad about it?"

"For God's sake, AJ, why would I be mad? It's not a big deal. So you gear up and do a few turns around the ice, take a couple swipes at the puck. So what?" He finally laughed at her reaction, a mixture of surprise and confusion.

"So you're not upset?"

"No AJ, I'm not upset. Did you really think I would be?" Again her gaze drifted downward. An icy rush of disbelief swirled through him, and his light mood from several minutes ago suddenly dimmed. "You honestly thought I would be mad about this? AJ, do you really think I'm that bad?"

"What? No. I just...I don't know. I didn't think you'd really be upset, but I didn't think you'd be jumping for joy, either."

"Why not?"

"Well...because...well, you weren't real thrilled about doing this whole thing to begin with, and the only reason you finally agreed to it was because of that bet. And I know for a fact that you didn't even think there was the slightest chance of you losing." Alec opened his mouth to disagree but she waved him off, obviously warming up to the conversation now. "And don't deny it. If you had thought there was even the slightest chance of me scoring, you'd have never agreed to it."

Alec sat back and twirled the wine glass between his fingers. She was right, of course, and it would be foolish for him to even pretend otherwise. But he couldn't complain about how things had turned out. Well, except for his initial shock at being blindsided by the first feature last week. But that had more to do with bad timing than anything else.

So no, he certainly had nothing to complain about. And if he had the chance to do it over again, he would.

So tell her, he thought. Alec lifted his head to meet her gaze, trying not to smile at her dismayed expression. "You're right, I probably wouldn't have. That doesn't mean I regret it."

AJ's eyes actually widened, if only for a fraction of a second. Then a light blush colored her cheeks and she quickly looked away, clearing her throat. He knew instantly what she was thinking, and spoke up before her mind went into overload conjuring up all the wrong reasons.

"And no, I wasn't talking about the sex. I don't regret that, either—I really, *really* don't regret that—but that's not what I meant."

"Then what did you mean?"

What did he mean? Alec sipped his wine, thinking. What was it Ian had said earlier? Oh yeah: AJ was his girlfriend. But it didn't feel like that. They didn't get dressed up and meet for dates, they didn't go dancing or out to dinner or circle around each other, trying to find hidden meanings in every word and gesture, out-doing themselves as they tried to impress the other.

They didn't do any of the agonizing things that Alec usually associated with dating today. Which was why he didn't date.

Alec frowned into his wine glass. Now that he was actually thinking about it, he realized that they didn't really do anything at all. The one time he had taken her out, it had been to a strip club. Of all places. Yeah, they hung out. Watched television and maybe a movie. She came to his practices and games.

He looked at the pizza tray in the middle of the table. They didn't even have nice meals—they had pizza, instead.

And—oh yeah—they slept together.

AJ wasn't his girlfriend. She was more like one of the guys on the team that he hung out with, except he was screwing her.

"Alec...so what did you mean?"

He looked up and noticed AJ staring at him, confusion creasing her brow, and he tried to remember what they had been talking about. Yeah, he remembered—why he didn't regret the bet. He drained his glass and cleared his throat. "I just meant that I like having you around, you know? I enjoy when we hang out."

Inwardly, he groaned. Those had to be the lamest words a man had ever said to a woman he liked. He reached for the bottle of wine and poured himself another glass, doing his best to not look at AJ. His resolve lasted for three seconds before he lifted his eyes to her face, expecting to see...well, he didn't know what he expected but it wasn't the sardonic half-smile and raised eyebrows aimed his way.

"Gee, Kolchak, I like you, too."

"I didn't mean—"

"I know. I actually kinda like hanging out with you, too. It hasn't been as bad as I thought it would be." AJ smiled, then quickly grimaced and looked away. Alec knew instantly the grimace had nothing to do with their losing conversation, and everything to do with her headache. He pushed his chair back and walked around the table, reaching for her hand and pulling her up.

"Go upstairs and lay down. I'll clean up down here and be up in a few minutes."

"No, I'm okay. Besides, you cooked, I should clean."

"AJ, no arguments. Go lay down before the headache turns into a migraine."

"It's not—"

Alec leaned forward and kissed her, stopping her in mid-sentence, enjoying the way she automatically leaned into him, enjoying her soft sigh against his lips, the tiny moan of disappointment when he pulled away. "No arguments. Now go."

He gently pushed her out of the dining room, then leaned against the door frame, enjoying her rear view as she made her way to the stairs. She turned around and gave him a small smile, as if she knew exactly what he had been doing as she walked away.

"Thanks Alec. And thanks for the dinner, too. It was sweet." She turned and walked upstairs, leaving him standing there, stunned.

He pushed away from the door frame, frowning. Sweet? Had she just called him sweet? That hadn't been what he was shooting for.

Alec turned and surveyed the dining room. Candles, music, wine. Pizza. So okay, maybe the pizza was a bit out there, but still...Sweet?

He bit his tongue and began clearing the table, his mind whirling. He didn't want her to feel like one his buddies, and he didn't want her to think he was sweet. So what did he have to do to change things?

He had no idea.

FOURTEEN

AJ stood at center ice and rolled her shoulders, trying to adjust the fit of the pads as she fought off a sense of déjà vu. A photographer stood off to the side, leaning against the player's bench as he spoke with Tim. She still couldn't believe her editor was here. Hell, she couldn't believe he had come up with this insane idea. Part of her wanted to shoot a puck in his direction and hope it hit him upside the head. Another part—the largest part—just wanted to go home and soak in the hot tub.

Wait. *She* didn't have a hot tub at home. The hot tub was at Alec's. And since when did she start thinking of his place as home?

She turned her head toward the end zone and studied Alec, leaning casually against the net as he talked to Ian. Her heart did a quick drum roll in her chest and she mentally kicked herself. What had she gotten into? And she wasn't talking about this whole photo shoot fiasco. She wasn't even talking about the exclusive feature articles. A few weeks ago, all she could think of was getting her by-line on an exclusive, of the excitement and sense of accomplishment she would feel at reaching that goal. Somehow the excitement wasn't as great she thought it would be now that she had actually done it.

In fact, the excitement pretty much paled in comparison to what she felt each night sleeping in Alec's arms. Just like last night, when she had come home—gone to Alec's, she corrected herself—and he surprised her with the dinner. She couldn't believe how much the sweet and thoughtful gesture had actually meant to her.

It shouldn't have meant nearly as much to her as it did. And the fact that it did, just like the fact that she was beginning to think of Alec's place as "home", was bad news. Really bad news. As in starting with "L" bad news.

AJ's stomach did a slow roll as her eyes again rested on Alec. He must have sensed her gaze on him because he turned toward her and smiled. In the brief moment that she allowed her eyes to meet his, enough heat seared through her that she was surprised she wasn't standing in a puddle of water from melting the ice.

She was so thoroughly screwed. How could she have let this happen? He was Alec Kolchak, for crying out loud. They had done nothing but bicker during every encounter they had ever had since first meeting several years ago. What had changed?

Maybe it wasn't the capital "L" trouble. Maybe it was just the capital "S" trouble. Because yeah, the sex was absolutely phenomenal. So maybe that was it. It had nothing to do with that "L" mess, it was just about the sex.

Yeah, sure. And maybe she wouldn't make an ass out of herself during this stupid photo shoot. She still didn't know what Tim had been thinking. Was it really necessary to have a picture of her on the ice for next week's feature? No, it wasn't. Not as far as she was concerned, anyway. She had more important things to worry about...like convincing herself she was *not* in love with Alec Kolchak.

"AJ, you almost ready?" Tim called from the player's bench. She jumped, startled, then turned and gave him as dirty a look she could get away with, which was pretty extreme. He either couldn't see her that well, or didn't care, because he didn't say anything, just eyed her impatiently.

Like he was the one standing on display out in the middle of the ice, getting ready to make an ass out of himself.

"Yeah, I'm ready." She tapped the blade of her stick on the ice and skated around in a small circle, then pushed off toward the player's bench. She wished she was skilled enough to stop with a spray of ice, but she didn't want to push her luck so she settled on just gliding to a stop near the boards. "Now what, exactly, is it you want me to do? Because I'm not really sure why everyone else is here."

Maybe "everyone else" was overstating it a bit. Besides Alec and Ian, there were three other players on the ice, including Jean-Pierre Larocque and Randy Michaels, hanging out near the penalty box looking mostly bored. The Banners' owner and General Manager were also present along with some other suits, all seated up in the stands and looking mildly interested.

And, of course, there were the fans and spectators who always showed up at practices, hoping to meet the players and get autographs. Not to mention the rink bunnies, who always hoped for more. There seemed to be more of the latter present today, which bothered AJ for some reason.

Probably because more than a few of the rink bunnies were eyeing Alec like he was an all-you-can-eat salad buffet. Nope, she couldn't imagine why that bothered her at all.

"AJ, are you even listening?"

She turned toward Tim and gave him an innocent look, which got her an eye roll and sigh in return. He pinched the bridge of his nose and muttered something under his breath, shook his head, then looked up at her.

"I want some shots of you actually playing. So just go out on the ice and skate around and hit the puck and Joey will take the pictures. Joey, make sure you get shots of the other players as well. We'll look at everything when we get back and go from there."

"Wait. The other players, too? You want me to actually, you know, play hockey? With these guys? For real?"

"Well what did you think I wanted?"

"I don't even know why you want pictures at all, so I didn't give it much thought. I just figured you wanted some shots of me skating around the ice or something."

"Exactly. Now go, do something." Tim made shooing motions with his hands then muttered something to Joey as she skated away. AJ could have sworn she heard someone yell out to make it look real, but when she turned back around, everybody seemed to be busy doing something else.

Shaking off a sense of impending disaster, she skated back to center ice, not surprised to see Ian meet her at the face-off circle. He offered her a slight smile and a wink, then dropped the puck between them.

"Ready on three?"

"Oh God, are we really doing this for real? Seriously? Please don't hurt me."

Ian chuckled as he placed the blade of his stick against the ice, waiting for her to do the same. AJ sighed then moved into position, noticing Joey sliding closer toward them, the camera to his eye. She let out a deep breath and listened for Ian's count, then scrambled for the puck. She muttered to herself when he slapped it away, then skated after it, knowing she had absolutely no chance of ever catching up to him.

Ian looked back over his shoulder at her and made some kind of motion with his hand. She didn't understand at first, then realized he was letting her know he was passing it to her a second before the puck flew her way.

AJ let it ease into her stick, then turned on the ice and skated toward the net, not caring if Joey was getting his pictures or not. Five feet from the net, she drew back with her stick and slammed the puck toward Alec.

Who, of course, deftly caught it without having to move so much as an inch. He winked at her then tossed the puck back out to the ice.

"C'mon sweetheart, you can do better than that."

AJ skidded to a stop in front of the net and stared at Alec, her eyes wide in feigned shock. "Sweetheart? No, you did not. Did you just 'sweetheart' me?"

Alec shrugged, a lopsided grin on his face. "It was either 'sweetheart' or 'babe'. I kind of liked 'sweetheart' but 'babe' works for me, too...babe."

"Oh no. No, you did not." AJ shook her head, biting back her smile as she reached out for the puck. He winked at her again then pulled his helmet back down.

"C'mon, sweetheart, show them what you've got."

AJ laughed then skated away from the net, passing the puck to Ian, who passed it to Randy. They continued playing for at least thirty minutes, giving AJ every chance to shoot. Not a single shot got by Alec, but she didn't care—she was having too much fun. Even when Jean-Pierre tried to get the puck away from her, and "accidentally" ran into her, sending her flying across the ice on her butt so he could race over and eagerly help her back up. The only thing that wasn't fun were the heated words exchanged between Alec and Jean-Pierre after that, but even that incident was quickly quelled by Ian's calm interference.

Tim finally called a halt to the mock "game", saying that Joey had enough photographs for them to go through. AJ had no idea what Tim was hoping for, or how he was even planning on using the pictures, but she wasn't going to argue. A half hour on the ice was enough to drain her.

Because, for as much fun as she was having, her body was ready to call it quits. Her arms were sore, her shoulders hurt, her legs were rubber, and she was drenched in sweat. Even her hands hurt. She had no idea how the players did this for real, night after night, and knew without hesitation that she was going to use this in next week's article. The details were still vague, but she was definitely going to use it.

AJ watched Tim and Joey head toward the suits in the stands, and let out a deep breath, grateful they were no longer paying much attention. With a heavy sigh, she lowered herself to the ice and laid flat on her back, closing her eyes and groaning as the muscles in her body stretched and screamed. No more than a few seconds went by before she heard the scrape of metal on ice near her head, and felt a presence hovering over her.

"What are you doing?"

"Dying."

"Not funny. C'mon, get up. All you're going to do by laying there is cramp up."

"Too late. I don't think I can move."

"Yeah you can. If you don't, I'll be forced to call you 'sweetheart' again."

AJ cracked open one eye and stared up at Alec, feeling her heart squeeze tightly at his teasing grin, at the warmth in his dark eyes. She closed her eyes again and cursed beneath her breath. *Too late* was an understatement.

"C'mon, up you go." She felt a pair of hands grab her right arm, then opened her eyes in surprise when a second pair grabbed her left arm. Ian was also standing next to her, laughing quietly as they pulled her to a standing position. She didn't even bother to try skating away, just let them pull her across the ice. Which was a good thing, since she didn't think she could really do more than just stand anyway.

"I think my legs have turned into Silly Putty."

"You'll get used to it. You actually did pretty good out there," Ian told her. She looked over at him, waiting for him to add something else, but only saw grudging admiration on his face.

"If you say so. I didn't even score once, though." She paused and gave Alec a mock dirty look. "The least you could have done was make it look like you had to work at least a little to make a few of those saves! It would have made the aches and pains more worth it."

Both men laughed again, still pulling her across the ice. Alec crooked his hand further through her elbow and pulled her just a little closer. "I'll make it up to you later. After we get home and you take a soak in the hot tub."

AJ's heart tripped in her chest and she stumbled just the smallest bit as they walked off the ice. *Don't read into it,* she told herself. He didn't mean it the way it sounded, she was sure of it. It was just a figure of speech, a meaningless phrase.

Ian reached behind him to slam the door shut, momentarily throwing her off balance since he still had hold of her arm. Alec's own hold tightened and she turned her face toward his, surprised to see him leaning toward her, as if he was getting ready to kiss her. Her heart hammered some more then she noticed a flash from the corner of her eye, and knew that Joey was back with his camera.

But she didn't understand why he was using a flash. AJ turned her head away from Alec, then felt herself being pushed to the side as a blur and another flash exploded in her vision. She stumbled and went down on one knee, almost taking Ian down with her.

She was saved from doing a full face plant right there in front of everyone only because Ian tightened his hold on her and quickly pulled her upright. Alec had let go of her other arm, and she turned to see what was going on.

Her body stiffened in disbelief. Alec had let go of her because he now had his arms full of a buxom blonde—one of the rink bunnies AJ had noticed earlier. Only maybe she wasn't a rink bunny, since Alec seemed to know her. At least, AJ thought he knew her, since he wasn't doing anything to push her away as she pressed against him.

"Alec! Have you missed me?"

AJ watched in stunned silence as the blonde wrapped her arms around Alec's neck then actually wrapped one leg around his before leaning forward and kissing him.

And it wasn't just a simple kiss, either. It was a full-contact, tongue-down-his-throat spectacle. AJ closed her mouth with an audible snap and just stared as the kiss continued, both parties apparently oblivious.

Oblivious to the small crowd. Oblivious to the attention they were drawing. Oblivious to the camera that was clicking and flashing away inches from them.

"Shit." The word may have come from her, but she thought it was most likely uttered by Ian. AJ pulled her arm from his grasp and turned away, making her way to the locker room. She ignored the sound of her name being called, focusing only on getting away from the unfolding scene, and barely registered the sight of Gerry Brown standing smugly off to the side. She paused, then shook her head and moved on, no longer caring about anything but getting away.

FIFTEEN

When it came to making a grand exit, AJ was an abject failure.

She had the entire scene planned: it would be mature, quiet, positive. Professional, even. And, hopefully, leave Alec-the-jerk feeling like a lowlife as she waltzed out the door with her bag and laptop in tow.

In reality, grand exits lost a lot of their drama when the person doing the exiting fell asleep with a wet head and only a partially-packed bag. And grand exits really lost all their appeal when the person doing the exiting had to be awakened by the person being exited.

Those were the incoherent, groggy thoughts that floated through AJ's head as she slowly came awake in the dim room. A few long seconds passed as she pushed herself to a sitting position and glanced around, trying to remember where she was.

Oh yeah. She was in Alec's guest bedroom. She had driven here after the fiasco following the photo shoot and packed most of her stuff, intending to just leave. The creeping soreness throbbing through her muscles had convinced her to at least take a shower so she wasn't completely miserable. Then she had stretched out on the bed, intending only to stretch, and had promptly fell asleep.

She pushed her tangled hair out of her face and eased herself out of the bed with a stifled groan, ignoring Alec as he leaned against the doorway and watched her. She threw her few remaining clothes into her duffle bag and zipped it shut, then stiffly walked across the room, stopping when Alec refused to move out of her way.

"Where are you going?"

AJ looked up at him and wondered why he even bothered to ask the question. Maybe the earlier kiss had melted what few brain cells she had given him credit for having.

"I'm going home."

"Why?"

"Why? Did you really just ask me why? Why do you think?"

"I don't know. That's why I'm asking."

AJ gritted her teeth and tried to push past him, only to have his arms close around her. She stiffened in his hold, refusing to budge, refusing to look up at him. She just stood there, only barely resisting the urge to swing her duffle bag upside his head, and then only because she didn't think she'd be able to lift it that far.

"Aren't you even going to ask me who she is?"

If possible, AJ stiffened even more, her back teeth grinding so hard she expected them to crack under the pressure. Her lying words were clipped as she spoke. "It's not my business."

"It's not?"

"No, it is not." But oh, how she wanted it to be. She wanted to know exactly who the woman was, how well Alec knew her—although she figured she already knew the answer to that one—and what their relationship was. Then she wanted to know where the woman lived so she could find her and rake her eyes out of her skull. Then she wanted to come back and do the same thing to Alec.

"You're lying. You want to know."

AJ pushed against him and broke free from his hold, her suppressed hurt morphing into sudden anger. How dare he try to make light of it? Did he really think it was funny?

She gripped her duffel bag tighter and pushed past him and into the hallway, heading for the stairs. Alec followed her but she ignored him, wanting only to get downstairs and out the door.

"AJ, wait. AJ, c'mon. I was joking."

She paused at the bottom of the stairs and turned to look up at him. "Joking? Yeah. Ha ha. Real funny."

Alec jumped the last two steps then moved in front of her when she turned away from him. He placed his hands on her shoulders and leaned down, pushing his face closer to hers. "AJ, I'm sorry. Alright? I thought if I tried to make a joke of it, the whole thing wouldn't suck so much."

"Well, it didn't work. And like I said—it's not my business, so don't worry about it." She stepped away and Alec's hands dropped from her shoulders. They looked at each other for a long minute, and AJ tried to think of something to say to break the silence. Her mind came up blank. After all, what could she say?

She couldn't come out and tell him how she felt—she wasn't even sure how she felt herself, not really. And he had never said anything about how he felt, either. Yeah, he liked having her around. Not exactly a declaration, since she was pretty sure he liked having food around, too.

"Why don't you think it's your business?" Alec finally asked, his voice quiet. She looked into his eyes but they were carefully veiled, giving away nothing. She took a deep breath and looked away, shaking her head.

"Alec, it's not like...I mean..." She took another deep breath and adjusted her grip on the bag. "We're not together, okay? You don't answer to me, I don't answer to you. So if there's...you know, someone else...that's your business, not mine."

"We're not together? Then what are we, AJ? Hell, you share my bed every night. What exactly is it that we're doing here?"

She couldn't look at him, afraid he would be able to see too much in her eyes if she did. So she shook her head again and took a step back. "I guess we're just sleeping together. And we wouldn't even be doing that if not for your stupid bet."

"Stupid bet?"

"Yeah. You would have never given me even a minute of your time if not for the bet and you know it." AJ's breath hitched in her chest at the words, and at the harsh truth of them. Up until a month ago, it was all she could do just to get Alec to look at her, and then it was usually because he was looking over his shoulder as he ran away. It would have almost been funny how quickly things had changed...if not for how she really felt.

She glanced up at Alec and wished she hadn't. He was standing less than a foot away, staring at her, his body stiff, his face devoid of all emotion. "So the last few weeks were, what? Research? An extra inside scoop?"

"What!" AJ stepped back as if she had been slapped. And while Alec seemed completely drained of all emotion, hers boiled to the surface. "Is that what you really think? You honestly believe I could just...do that? Thanks, Kolchak. You just proved that you know absolutely nothing about me."

She turned her back on him and walked to the door, digging in the bowl he kept on the entranceway table for her keys. Her eyes closed and she counted to ten while taking deep breaths, searching for a rational calm she didn't feel. Alec was standing next to her when she opened her eyes, studying her, his face no longer quite so blank. But she still couldn't tell what he was thinking or feeling.

"AJ, that's not—"

"Listen, just...don't say anything, okay? I'm almost finished with the series and you're getting ready for an away stretch. The thirty days will be over before you get back so..." She shrugged and cleared her throat, looking away from Alec. "It's time for me to leave, anyway."

Saying the words out loud hurt her more than she thought they would, but she didn't know what else to do. She had known it would be too easy to become attached but she had let herself do it anyway, thinking...well, she hadn't been thinking. That was the whole problem.

Her hands closed around the keys and she squeezed her fist closed, not caring that the metal dug into her palm. When she looked up, Alec was still standing next to her, not moving, not doing much of anything. She wished he would say something to break the silence and at least make her feel less uncomfortable. It felt like a full minute dragged by before he finally nodded and stepped away. It wasn't quite what she was expecting or hoping for.

"Well, if the time is up, then I guess that's it." He took a step back, not really looking at her, his gaze focused somewhere over her shoulder. AJ stood motionless, pain tearing through her. Had she really thought he would declare his undying love for her? No.

But that didn't mean she hadn't hoped. Maybe not for an undying declaration, but certainly for something other than his obvious dismissal.

Alec looked back at her, his eyes distant, a slow ticking in his clenched jaw. "So tell me. Is it really because the time is up for the bet? Or is it something else?"

She swallowed and looked down at the keys in her hand, blinking hard several times, wondering what she should say. She finally looked up and shrugged. "I don't know. I mean...I don't know, Alec. You asked me what we're doing here. I could ask you the same thing. What do *you* think we're doing here? Because, you know, I'm not the one who was sucking face with some strange woman in front of reporters and spectators."

He watched her for a long minute then looked away with a small shake of his head. AJ's stomach clenched and her heart tightened in her chest. She took a deep breath, swallowed, then let the breath out in a rush. "Yeah, well. It's been fun, right? And it's not like we won't see each other again, so—"

"AJ, that's not—"

"No, really. It's not a big deal, you know? We're both adults and—"

"AJ—"

The shrill buzz of the doorbell echoed through the entranceway, silencing both of them. AJ met Alec's eyes, wishing she could read their dark depths. The doorbell buzzed again and Alec cursed as he stepped toward the door. "Damn shitty timing."

AJ was going to say something about him not having to answer it but her mouth snapped shut when he opened the door. Standing on the other side was the blonde from earlier, one hand resting high on the door frame, the other resting casually on her hip. The pose was so obviously deliberate.

And her appearance so very shocking that AJ actually sucked in her breath in surprise, feeling as if she had been slapped across the face. She couldn't see Alec's face, but she thought his back stiffened and she was pretty sure he was just as surprised at the blonde's appearance as she was.

Or maybe she just wanted to believe that. Because, once again, the blonde stepped forward and grabbed Alec in a full-body embrace and plastered her mouth against his.

AJ didn't bother to wait and see Alec's reaction; she leaned down to grab her bag and threw it over her shoulder, then pushed pass the lip-locked couple, not caring that she hit them with the bag. She pressed the button for the private elevator and muttered a sigh of thanks when the door opened immediately. Alec called her name but she ignored him and hit the button for the lobby before turning around, careful not to look up.

The door had just started to close when Alec raced in beside her, pushing her against the wall of the elevator with his solid body. "AJ, don't go."

The door closed with a hiss and AJ felt a second of panic at Alec's closeness. She shoved against him, staring at her hands splayed against the shirt pulled tight across his chest. His solid body didn't budge; instead, he stepped closer and cradled her face with his hands, forcing her to look up at him.

"AJ, don't go," he repeated, his voice just above a whisper. She finally raised her eyes to meet his, searching for something, an answer or an indication or...something. But the dark depths of his eyes revealed...nothing she could easily read.

"Alec, there's no reason for me to stay."

His mouth closed over hers in a searing kiss she didn't see coming, his lips claiming hers with a moist heat so intense that she fell against him with a soft sigh. Alec gentled the kiss too quickly, pulling away and resting his forehead against hers. "For this. Isn't this reason enough?"

AJ closed her eyes and took a deep breath. More than anything, she wanted to say yes. But for reasons more than deep kisses, passion, lust.

"Alec, I...no, it's not. I'm sorry." This time he took a step back when she pushed against him, his face carefully blank. The door opened and Alec placed his hand against the frame, his gaze holding hers. She searched her mind for something to say, anything, but came up with nothing. AJ told herself it was just as well, because she doubted if she could get any words past her thick throat.

She readjusted her grip on the bag and stepped past Alec, out of the elevator and into the lobby. She stood with her eyes closed for a second, then turned when she heard the doors begin to close. Alec stood motionless, his face blank as he stared at her. At the last possible second, just before the doors finally closed, an emotion flashed in the depths of his eyes, so briefly that AJ told herself it was merely a figment of her imagination, wishful thinking.

She took a deep breath, swallowed, and blinked hard, then turned and walked out of the lobby.

#

The paper landed in front of her with a loud rustle, covering the keyboard. AJ glanced down at it, clenched her jaw, and impatiently brushed it away, not bothering to look up at the person who threw it. The shadow grew larger, blotting out the light in her cubicle, and she let out a sigh of irritation.

"They make a nice couple, don't you think?"

AJ gritted her teeth again and took a deep breath, warning herself not to let her impatience—or anger—show. "If you say so."

Gerry Brown reached down for the paper and made a show of casually flipping through the pages. "I still don't know which picture is my favorite. There are so many to choose from. There's this one of them dressed up on the town..." The colorful pages rustled as he flipped through them. "Or this one of the happy couple reuniting at the rink..." More rustling, then a chuckle. "But I do think my favorite is this one here. It really captures your graceful side." The paper was tossed back on her keyboard, and she didn't have to look down to see which picture he was talking about. She had seen them all before, had their images branded on her retinas from staring at them in disbelief for so long.

Pictures of Alec and the rink bunny. Or rather, his once-ex-and-now-current girlfriend. Apparently happily reunited after not seeing each other for more than two years. AJ tried to convince herself that the expression on Alec's face looked more like constipation rather than happiness, but that was probably more wishful thinking.

The page Gerry had turned to showed another color picture from the photo shoot nearly two weeks ago: her sliding across the ice on her butt, just after Jean-Pierre had knocked into her during the mock game. She glanced down at it one last time then batted it away.

"How's it feel to sell your soul for a byline, Gerry? Proud of the tabloid trash?" The words were light and flippant, reflecting none of the anger that had been seething through her since the local tabloid had come out a few days ago.

Gerry reached down and snatched the paper away, a flush mottling his face. His hands crumpled the pages, the paper twisting in his fists as he leaned closer. "At least I didn't trade sex for a story and a paycheck."

AJ stood so fast that her desk chair slid into the cubicle wall with a bang. She stepped toward Gerry, effectively blocking his escape from the small area, and took grim satisfaction at the look of alarm that crossed his smarmy face.

"AJ, I need to discuss your next assignment in my office." Tim's cool voice stopped her from saying or doing anything, which was probably a good thing. She took a step backward and grabbed her planner off the desk, then shut down her laptop and tossed it into her bag, her eyes never leaving Gerry's.

He smirked at her, baring his shark-like teeth and sending a chill down her spine. He opened his mouth to say something, but Tim interrupted him. "And Gerry, you have a new assignment as well. Congratulations, you're now the community columnist for the monthly insert."

"What?" Gerry spun around, directing his outrage toward the editor. "That isn't even a full-time staff position!"

"Well, I'm sure you can supplement your income with more freelance ventures."

AJ tucked her chin into her chest and bit back a smile. As much as she wanted to gloat in Gerry Brown's face, she knew Tim would call her on it. That didn't mean she wasn't going to do a happy-dance later.

She hadn't had much to be happy about lately.

AJ followed Tim to his office, ignoring Gerry's sputters of indignation and tossed insults as he stormed away. Tim closed the door and motioned for her to have a seat, then perched on the edge of the desk and watched her with an unusually blank expression. AJ forced herself to sit still and meet his gaze head-on.

Tim nodded, as if satisfied with something, then grabbed a pencil from his desk and started tapping it against his leg. "Are you doing okay?"

The question caught her off-guard and she sat back a little, not knowing what to make of it. She finally nodded, a hesitant motion of her head, and watched him carefully.

"Good. Good. And, of course, you know better than to believe anything you read in the local rag, right? Of course you do. Good, good."

AJ continued staring at her usually forthright and outspoken editor, and wondered what was wrong with him. He, in turn, watched her back, studying her, and she felt like he was searching for...something. She was ready to ask him what was wrong when he bounded from the desk and walked around to his chair, flopping into it with a loud creak.

"I've got to hand it to you, AJ: you did a great job with the feature. People were impressed, and not just the readers. I'm still getting calls from the Banners' front office about it. Not to mention the calls from the other sports venues. It seems you really tapped into something. Congratulations, you should be proud of yourself."

AJ nodded again, not sure what to say. Of course she was proud. Of course the congratulations meant something to her. But Tim already knew that, because they had already had this conversation earlier in the week, right after the final installment ran.

"So how are you doing on that last assignment?"

The change in topic confused her for a split-second, but she finally nodded. "Almost done. I have an interview in the morning and expect to have the final draft by the afternoon."

"Good. I have another assignment for you. Let's call it a mini-feature. Are you up for another one so soon?"

"Tim, are you feeling okay?"

"What? Of course, why? Do I not look okay?"

"You look fine. I just don't understand what you're up to. Since when do you ask a staff writer if they're 'up to another assignment'? Of course I'm up to it. Who wouldn't be? It's my job now!" She bit back the brief smile at the pleasure saying that brought to her. It was her job. She had worked so hard for it.

The pleasure dimmed as the memories of that last day with Alec flashed through her mind, and she ruthlessly quashed them. They were both adults; they had both had fun while it lasted. Now she had her dream job.

And he had a new girlfriend. The bastard.

"Good, good. This is an easy one. A few days at the most." He rummaged through the pile on his desk, scattering papers before he found what he was looking for. "I already scheduled the interviews you'll need for Friday. Do you have any formal wear?"

AJ blinked, hard, having trouble following his fast speech. He had scheduled the interviews? Since when...the last part finally sunk in and she stared at him. "Formal wear? You mean, like a gown?"

"No, a tux. Of course I mean a gown. Or whatever it is women wear to these things. Do you have one?"

"Uh..."

"If you don't, that's alright. I'll have Mandy make an

appointment at Trendy Formals and they'll handle it. I would also suggest going to the salon and getting your hair and all that crap done on Saturday. I'll have Mandy make that appointment for you."

"Uh, Tim..."

"And I also took the liberty of arranging a date for you so—"

"Tim, stop!" Her voice was a borderline screech but she didn't care as long as it got his attention. Which, apparently, it did, because he finally stopped his rambling long enough to look at her. "Tim, what the hell exactly do you have me doing? Scheduled interviews, a gown, salon? A date? What's going on?"

Tim glanced around the office and shifted in his chair before he let out a deep breath and looked at her. "You're covering the Baltimore Ball Saturday night."

Silence filled the room as quickly as the chill that swept over her. The Baltimore Ball was a big charity event that showcased and awarded Charm City's sports players: baseball, football, basketball.

Ice hockey.

AJ's stomach did a slow roll as she concentrated on not clenching her fists. The yearly event was a black-tie, red-carpet affair that some compared to showy Hollywood events, and it drew all sorts of dignitaries and local celebrities.

And athletes. Let's not forget the athletes.

AJ took a deep breath, counted to ten, and let it out slowly, her gaze never leaving Tim's face. "Wouldn't this be something better-suited to one of the entertainment columnists? I mean, it's always been covered that way before, I don't remember a sports writer ever covering it—"

"There will be a feature writer there from the entertainment section—"

"So then why are you sending me?"

"The Banners suggested—rather strongly—that it would be a great follow-up and that you would be the best choice." He paused, took a deep breath, and spoke the next words in a rush. "Since Alec Kolchak is supposed to receive some kind of award."

AJ clenched both her jaw and her fists, and made no attempt to hide it. As much as she might want to, she couldn't say no. Even if she thought she could convince Tim otherwise—and she wasn't foolish enough to even try—to say no would negate everything she had done, everything she had worked so hard for. So big deal. She would have to see Alec again. She could handle the discomfort for a few hours.

AJ did another slow count and slowly relaxed her closed fists. She pasted on a big smile and blinked at Tim. "So, you said you lined up a date. Why? And who?"

Tim shifted in the chair and at least had enough sense to look momentarily uncomfortable. "Considering...the situation...I thought you might be more comfortable with a date than by yourself. I can certainly cancel it if that's what you want."

"Who?"

"Um..." He glanced down at the paper in his hands, squinted, then looked up at her. "Ian Donovan. He's...well, I guess you know who he is."

"Ian? Great. Perfect. You picked one of Alec's friends and teammates. This could be fun. So does Ian know?"

"Yes, he does. He was actually excited at the idea."

"Yeah, I bet." She could only imagine what he really thought. A grimace crossed her face; on second thought, she was probably better off not imagining what he really thought.

"Do you think you'll have any problems with this?"

AJ narrowed her eyes at him, then leaned across the desk and snatched the paper from his hands. "None at all."

She shoved the sheet of paper into her bag and left the office, wondering what the hell she had just gotten into.

SIXTEEN

AJ hiked the backpack higher on her shoulder and let out a loud sigh as she hurried toward the exit door of the practice rink. She was careful to hug the side of the wall, as far from the ice—and the players—as possible. Practice was still going on, so she figured she was as safe as she could be from running into anybody.

No, not anybody. Alec.

The urge to turn around and look, to watch him at the far end of the ice, was so strong that she almost gave into it. Almost...until she took a closer look at the crowd gathered around the boards and saw the blonde standing there.

AJ gritted her teeth and kept walking, mentally counting the steps to freedom and cursing Tim for scheduling the interviews at the practice rink offices during the actual practice. It didn't matter that the timing was logical; she wasn't in a rational mood.

She was several yards from the doors, from freedom, when she heard her name being called. Her first instinct was to bolt for the exit but she caught herself at the last second, realizing that the voice was different, the cadence and rhythm of her name not quite the same.

AJ took a deep breath and stopped, then slowly turned around to see Ian shuffling toward her in that odd off-ice gait. She adjusted her bag once more and offered him a small smile.

"Hey Ian."

"Hey." His long-legged stride closed the distance, quickly bringing him to her side. He shifted his stick from one hand to the other and back again, acting as if he was nervous. She could only imagine why, and decided to give him his out.

"Listen, about tomorrow night—"

"Yeah, I was going to call you later for the details—"

"You don't have to...I mean, I appreciate it and all, but you didn't have to agree and—" Ian interrupted her with a shake of his head, and wrapped his hand in a gentle grip around her arm and pulled her a few steps off to the side, glancing over his shoulder before lowering his head closer.

"I know, but I think it's a good idea. Besides, I didn't have a date, so you'll actually be doing me a favor."

AJ raised her brows at him, letting him know without words that she wasn't buying it. No matter what he said, she was going to feel like this was an agreement made out of pity, and she didn't want that. She opened her mouth to tell him she really didn't think it was a good idea, but he interrupted her again with a shake of his head.

"No arguments." He shifted his weight on his skates and glanced over his shoulder again, a small grin of satisfaction on his face. "Listen, I don't want to go to this thing, period. And I really don't want to go by myself. I don't think you do, either. Besides, I really think it would be a good idea for someone else to see you with a date. It might knock some sense into him."

His words stopped her cold, freezing her in place. That exact thought had been hovering at the edge of her subconscious, fighting to be recognized and acknowledged. Yes, some deep part of her hoped for the same thing; not necessarily to knock sense into Alec, but, just maybe, just a little bit, to make him jealous.

She didn't want to admit that she was that petty, though. "Ian, I appreciate it, I really do. But I don't think—"

He leaned in closer, his mouth inches from her ear, and AJ knew that anyone watching would think they were sharing more than just a casual moment. "I do. Trust me, Alec is miserable but won't admit it. But he's too damn thick-headed to fix things on his own."

"Then that's his own problem, and nothing I do is going to matter."

Ian glanced over his shoulder again then turned back to face her, a mischievous twinkle in his eyes. "Do you honestly believe that?"

The expression on his face almost made her take a step

backward, because it was obvious he was up to something. And she had a strong feeling that whatever it was wasn't going to be good. But she held her ground. "Yeah, I do."

"Play along and I'll prove you wrong."

"Wha—" AJ didn't get a chance to finish her sentence; Ian pulled her to him and lowered his mouth to hers so fast she didn't have time to talk, let alone react. One second he had been grinning at her then, before she realized what he was doing, his lips had claimed hers in a warm, gentle kiss.

Her first stunned thought was that his lips were soft and warm. Her next thought was...that he definitely wasn't Alec. Alec's kisses were fire and heat and passion and magic. Kissing Alec was like breathing life, like the first drop of a fast roller coaster or free-falling from a cliff; kissing Ian was like...eating vanilla ice cream or riding a small merry-go-round: nice, but kind of plain and, well, not very exciting.

Ian slowly pulled away but didn't let her go, just smiled down at her with that twinkle still in his eyes. "Good thing I have a healthy ego or your reaction would crush me."

"Ian, I'm—"

"No, don't say anything. Just give me a hug and look over my shoulder." He pulled her closer again, giving her no choice but to do as he said. The backpack slipped from her shoulder and jerked her arm downward, making the hug feel even more awkward. Still, she played along, wrapping her arms mostly around his waist as she looked behind him.

Alec was stepping off the ice, his helmet pushed up to reveal a forbidding scowl on his face. He reached behind him and slammed the rink door so hard that an unnatural echo bounced off the ice and shot around them. The look in his eyes darkened as his eyes met and locked on hers, and his gait quickened as he headed their way.

She stiffened in Ian's arms and tried to pull back, but he wouldn't completely release her, easing his hold only enough that she could look up at him without hurting herself. To her surprise, he was on the verge of laughing, and she could tell he was struggling not to.

"Do you still think that what you do doesn't matter to him?"

"Oh my God, he's furious! He looks like he's ready to hit both of us!" Her initial surprise at both Ian's kiss and Alec's reaction quickly changed to irritation. Alec was storming toward them, dark anger clear on his face. Like he had a right to be angry. AJ clenched her jaw and stared at him. "What is his problem? He's acting like...like...like a freaking caveman!"

"That's my girl! So, quick, before he kicks my ass—are we on for tomorrow night?"

AJ stepped out of Ian's arms and looked up at him with a bright smile. "You absolutely better believe we're on for tomorrow!"

Alec reached them just as she stepped away from Ian, and there was no doubt that he had heard her. His dark gaze drifted from her to Ian, then finally back to her, pinning her in place. She saw his hand tighten on his stick and noticed the slight tick in his clenched jaw as he gave her a curt nod.

"AJ. I didn't know you were going to be here today."

She did her best to keep her expression carefully blank but she wasn't sure she succeeded, especially when her gaze darted off to the side where Alec's girlfriend was now carefully watching the scene. AJ pulled her gaze away and looked at Alec, then at Ian. He gave her the slightest nod and a wink she knew Alec couldn't see. The encouragement boosted her determination, and she reached out to place her hand on Ian's arm, giving it a small squeeze of thanks as she looked back at Alec.

"I'm sorry, Alec, but I didn't realize I had to get your okay before working."

"Working?" His cold gaze swept over her and Ian, and he raised his brow in obvious disbelief. "Let me guess, it's Ian's turn to be...interviewed."

AJ clenched her jaw as hurt ripped through her with a searing heat that flushed her cheeks. She was speechless, and felt herself floundering for something, anything, to say. Ian jumped to her rescue even as Alec's face cleared enough for him to manage to look like he was sorry. Ian didn't wait for him to say anything, he just turned and pushed against Alec hard enough to make him stumble.

"Hey, *asshole*, you're way out of line."

"I—"

"What the hell gives you the right to talk to her like that? Who the hell do you think you are?" Ian kept advancing on Alec, forcing him back a bit at a time. And AJ realized Ian wasn't pretending—he was truly pissed, and on her behalf.

She also realized that Alec wasn't going to push back, that he was going to quietly accept whatever Ian dished out. And from what she could see of Ian's face, he was just getting started.

AJ blinked against the burning in her eyes and swallowed against the thickness in her throat, half-tempted to just turn around and leave. But she couldn't. As much as she wanted to, she couldn't. So she stepped forward and placed her hand on Ian's arm, surprised at the tension thrumming through the hard muscles. She squeezed, just the smallest bit, to get his attention.

"Ian, don't worry about it. Really, it's not a big deal." Both men turned to face her, their expressions unreadable. She glanced at Alec, for just a second, then turned her attention back to Ian. "Ian, I mean it. C'mon. Just let it go."

The two men continued staring at each other, one looking like he wanted to be tossed around, and the other looking like he would be more than happy to oblige. AJ squeezed Ian's arm again, then tugged on it. Ian finally looked down at her, then grabbed her hand and clasped it in his before turning and leading her away from the unfolding drama. He stopped and looked back, his jaw clenching as he gave Alec an undecipherable look.

"I never pegged you as a loser, Kolchak." Ian motioned to the side with his head, and AJ leaned past him to see what he was pointing at. The blonde was sauntering toward them, wobbling on stiletto heels that were sinking into the rubber mat. She reached Alec and pressed herself against him, wrapping possessive hands around his arms as she dropped a cool look in AJ's direction.

AJ barely refrained from rolling her eyes as Ian led her away from them. He stopped just before they reached the door and looked down at her, his eyes thoughtful but, thankfully, not pitying.

"So, see you tomorrow night?" Ian asked. AJ nodded, offering him a small smile. He leaned down to give her a quick kiss then straightened and smiled back. "Good. I'll pick you up at six o'clock."

"Why so early?"

"Because it's a team tradition to go for cocktails and real food before the dinner and awards. Are you still up for it?"

"Sure, why not. Count me in."

Ian laughed and pushed the door open for her, and she realized that he didn't believe her. Probably because the lack of enthusiasm she felt echoed in her weak words. She gave him one last small smile then walked out of the rink, trying not to pay any attention to the goalie who still stood behind Ian, staring at her instead of paying attention to the woman glued to his side.

#

AJ tried not to wiggle in the leather seat, knowing that it would probably wrinkle the gown she was wearing. Worse than wrinkle; it would probably tear along the side-seam and create an even bigger slit than was already there.

Not that it would take much to do that, if you asked her. But nobody had, and now she was stuck wearing this stupid gown. The stupid, stupid gown she should have said 'no' to. She took that back; she should have done more that just said 'no'—she should have stomped her foot and thrown a full-blown temper tantrum when both Tim and his secretary and the idiot clerk at Trendy Formals all insisted that the gown was made for her.

But she hadn't, and now she was stuck. And if Ian's reaction when he picked her up was any indication, she was going to be uncomfortable all night long. Which was bound to make an already-long night even more miserable.

She finally let out a loud sigh and turned away from the window to face Ian, not bothering to hide her frustration. "Why do you keep staring at me?"

The poor man obviously hadn't expected the question, because he jerked his gaze up to meet hers and started stammering, a small blush creeping across his face. If not for how his reaction was making her feel, she would almost feel sorry for him. Or at least maybe find something to laugh about in the whole sorry situation.

But she wasn't feeling much compassion or humor right now.

"I'm sorry, I really am. I just...wow. You just...you have no idea..."

"Okay, that's it. I can't do this." Her hands tightened on the miniscule bag that was supposed to serve as a purse. "Just, take me home. This whole thing was a stupid idea. I can't—"

"AJ, stop. I'm sorry." Ian moved and settled himself next to her, turning so they faced each other. His hands clasped both of hers and he offered her a sheepish grin. "I really am sorry. I didn't mean to make you uncomfortable. It's just...when you answered the door dressed like that, like this...you caught me off guard. I mean, you've always looked nice but you've always been dressed, you know, normal. And you look great. You really do. I mean, wow, you have no idea—"

"Stop! You're not making me feel any better!" She pulled her hands from his and tried to turn in the seat, but was afraid of moving too quickly for fear of tearing the gown. Or dislodging it.

The gown had looked beautiful when she saw it in the shop, a shimmering copper silk that caught her eyes and screamed for her attention. And it felt beautiful, rich and elegant, when she tried it on. And she had been so certain that it would look good, too.

Right up until she had turned around to look at herself in the mirror and saw how much flesh the gown exposed—and accentuated. Not even the small wrap that came with it had enough material to completely cover her.

It was then that she had said "no"...and been promptly overruled by everyone around her.

"AJ, you're beautiful." Ian's quietly spoken words, issued in a hush surrounded by the plush interior of the limousine, caught her attention and she turned back to face him. The smoldering look of appreciation in his eyes surprised her. Surprised—and panicked.

"Ian—"

He sat back and laughed, a short sound of frustration and humor. "AJ, if I thought there was even the slightest chance that you were interested, I would try. But I know better. Trust me, I will be the perfect gentleman tonight, so don't worry. And you *are* beautiful. If Alec isn't smart enough to come to his senses after tonight, then you deserve better."

AJ swallowed against the thickness that had formed in her throat at his heartfelt words, then offered him a small smile in thanks. She was going to be self-conscious no matter what Ian said, but maybe she really was overreacting. So the gown was more revealing than what she was accustomed to. So what? It was still beautiful. And yes, she could admit—at least to herself—that she felt beautiful. Between the gown, the jewelry and accessories, the hair, and the makeup—all carefully chosen, coifed, and applied—she almost felt like Cinderella going to the ball. She was living every girl's princess fantasy.

Except her Prince Charming was really Prince Chump who

was taking someone else to the ball.

And was she really sitting her, all dressed up in the back of a limo, comparing herself to Cinderella? What had gotten into her? She mentally shook her head to snap out of it. This wasn't a ball, this was work. She had an actual job to do tonight. Yes, she could try to have fun, but this was still about work.

The limo came to a stop in front of a row of refurbished and converted row homes, and AJ peered over Ian's shoulder to see where they were. Recognition came quickly, and she turned back to face him in laughing disbelief. "Canton? Seriously?" The trendy Baltimore neighborhood had been revitalized several years ago, and was now a mecca of popular night clubs and restaurants.

Ian shrugged and offered her a smile. "I never said the first part of the night was going to be fancy. But if you're worried about crowds, don't be. The Canton Club is ours for the duration—the team rents the entire place, so it's relatively private." He studied her, then offered her his hand as the driver opened the door for them. "Are you ready?"

AJ took a deep breath, then rested her hand in Ian's. "Ready as I'll ever be."

SEVENTEEN

Despite her initial misgivings, AJ was enjoying herself. For another ninety minutes, she was free to relax and just enjoy the evening.

Except that she had to stop her gaze from wandering around the crowded downstairs, searching for one hockey player out of the dozens that were already here. She tried telling herself she was merely enjoying watching everyone, dressed in tailored tuxedos and escorting dates wearing designer fashion gowns. And it wasn't just the hockey players in attendance; there were several players from Baltimore's football team as well as the baseball team. Apparently some light-hearted party crashing had occurred, which Ian told her was another tradition.

She glanced to her side and offered him another smile as he handed her a glass of wine, then cupped her elbow and led her away from the boisterous teasing that was going on right next to them. "Having fun so far?"

AJ sipped the wine then nodded. "Yes, believe it or not. Everyone looks so different, all dressed up."

"See? Now can you understand my reaction when I picked you up tonight?" Ian laughed and took a sip of his own drink, then stepped closer to her as a huge football player passed by. AJ's eyes widened in recognition as he walked by, and she nearly choked on the wine when the man briefly stopped and gave her an appreciative look. There was nothing dangerous or even lecherous about the look, just pure masculine appreciation, but AJ still felt just a little intimidated and stepped closer to Ian.

He chuckled and grabbed her elbow in a gentle grip to lead her into an adjoining room. This one wasn't as crowded or filled with as much noisy conversation as the other, due in part to the band that was set-up in the corner. "You should get used to drawing attention, especially tonight."

"What? Why?" AJ quickly glanced down at herself, wondering if she had spilled something on herself or, worse, if the gown had shifted.

"I told you: you are beyond beautiful. You'd be surprised at some of the comments the guys have made." He must have seen her look of horror because he quickly shook his head. "All good, don't worry. Now c'mon, let's dance."

He sat their drinks on a side table then led her onto the floor with the scattering of other couples already there. A slower song was playing, and Ian took her into his arms and led her through the steps of a slow dance. AJ let herself relax, allowing the din of conversation surrounding them disappear, allowing the stress of the last few weeks fade away for at least a little while.

Until Ian's shoulders tensed under her hands and he faltered for one small step. That tiniest movement, coupled with the sudden sensation of being watched, set off her internal alarm, and all the tension quickly came back. Ian's hand tightened briefly against her back, and he lowered his mouth to her ear. "Smile and relax, okay?"

She took a deep breath and forced a smile on her face, then laughed with genuine humor at Ian's grimace. The song faded to an end, and Ian clasped his hand around hers and led her off the floor. AJ tried not to look around for Alec, she really did, but her eyes had their own agenda and automatically sought him out, zeroing in on him without fail.

And while her eyes might have appreciated his appearance, actually seeing him standing there with his gaze focused completely on her almost made her stumble. Alec dressed down in jeans and a t-shirt was pulse-racing. Alec in uniform, playing on the ice, was jaw-dropping. Alec in work-out clothes was drool-worthy.

But Alec in a sleek tailored tux designed for his perfect form, his hair carelessly slicked back, his dark eyes slowly drifting over her...that was enough to cause all-out heart failure. And for one fraction of a second, for one-half of a heart beat, she thought he was going to approach her, that he was going to come toward her and take her in his arms and...

And then reality bitch-slapped her across the face because Alec wasn't alone. Of course he wasn't. His girlfriend sauntered in from the other room and dug her talons into his arm, turning up to face him with a Botox-enhanced pout.

With the sharp precision of a surgeon's knife, AJ accepted the fact that it was time to let go of whatever fantasy she may have still been nurturing. She may have thought she loved him—no, not thought, did—but it didn't matter. Even if there had ever been any chance at a real relationship between them—and she was beginning to admit that there probably hadn't been—that time was over.

She took a deep breath and offered Alec a small smile and nod of acknowledgement, then turned toward Ian. The expression on his face surprised her, and her own smile faltered. He was glaring at Alec, not even trying to hide his frustration and displeasure. She tugged on his hand to get his attention, then lifted her shoulders in a small shrug. "Ian, it's over. Really. We both made our choices. It's time to move on."

Ian turned to face her, his eyes unreadable as he studied her. And for one selfish second she wished that she really could move on, that she was the kind of woman who could bounce from one relationship—one man—to the next. Because Ian was extremely attractive, and if things were different, maybe she could actually be interested in him.

Except she felt only friendship for him.

He must have been able to read her mind; either that, or her thoughts showed too clearly on her face because his expression cleared and he laughed, a warm chuckle that made her smile in return. He draped his arm around her shoulder and pulled her close, then dropped a kiss on her forehead and led her deeper into the room, away from Alec and his date.

He paused on the way to the bar and leaned over to Jean-Pierre Larocque, saying something in a low voice that AJ didn't catch. She was going to ask him, but the band started playing again, an upbeat dance version of a popular hit, and Ian quickly detoured so they were back on the dance floor.

Thirty minutes later and AJ laughingly begged for mercy, shaking her head when the massive football player who had noticed her earlier tried to keep her out on the floor for another dance. At least now she had an idea of what Ian had said to his teammate earlier, because she had been kept on the dance floor by one player or another for the last half-hour. It didn't matter what song was playing, she had a dance partner that kept her moving, that kept her talking and laughing.

That kept her mind off the goalie standing in the corner, glowering. Not that anybody else except his date was paying much attention to him. In fact, it seemed that everyone was going out of their way to pointedly ignore Alec and his date.

And AJ was too petty to feel sorry for him, and too human not to get at least a little perverse pleasure out of it.

She finally made her way back to Ian and gratefully accepted the glass he held out to her, greedily drinking the ice water and catching her breath. He motioned toward the bartender then replaced her empty water glass with a full wine glass.

"Are you having fun?"

"Yes, I am. And thank you."

"For what?"

AJ raised her brows at him, letting him know that he couldn't get away with acting innocent. She placed her hand on his arm and leaned closer so she wouldn't have to shout. "For making sure I'm having fun. For making sure that there's always someone ready to dance with me."

Ian continued looking confused, and shook his head at her. "I have no idea what you think I did—"

"Ian, I'm not completely oblivious. I know you said something to Jean-Pierre to make sure Alec was ignored and that I was kept busy on the dance floor."

"AJ, really, I didn't—" Ian stopped and glanced at something behind her then grabbed her hand and started leading her away. "But dancing seems like—"

"Excuse me."

AJ stiffened as the voice from behind her cut through the conversation and music around them. It wasn't loud. In fact, she doubted if anyone else besides her and Ian had even heard the soft interruption. But the sound echoed in her mind and caused her heart to speed up. Her stomach rolled from nervousness, trepidation, and anticipation, and it seemed as if every person in the room had stopped to watch.

Which was just her ridiculous imagination, of course. There was nothing to watch, nothing to anticipate, nothing to be nervous about. AJ took a deep steadying breath and slowly turned around, keeping her face carefully blank as Alec gazed at her.

"AJ, I was wondering if you'd like to—" Alec motioned to the dance floor behind him and cleared his throat. "Would you care to dance?"

She felt Ian's eyes on her, along with the stares of several other players who were nearby, and knew that all she had to do was shake her head. If she did that, she knew that Alec wouldn't bother her the rest of the night, that he wouldn't even be able to get close to her.

She opened her mouth to say 'no', but there was a flash of something in Alec's eyes that changed her mind. She didn't know what she had seen—or thought or even hoped she had seen—but she found herself giving him a simple nod before she could think better of it.

Alec took the wine glass from her, his eyes never leaving hers as he handed it off to someone before guiding her out to the floor with a gentle hand placed in the small of her back. She was still reeling from the heat of that small touch against her bare skin when Alec pulled her into his arms as the band started a Jason Aldean/Kelly Clarkson duet. AJ stumbled when she recognized the song, wishing they had played something different.

Because she was very much afraid that if Alec asked her did she want stay, she would foolishly say yes.

But as Alec wrapped his hand around hers and drew it against his chest, as his other hand rested low and warm against her back, she realized that it didn't matter what song the band played. Because any song would bring her too close to Alec.

AJ stiffened and tried to put some distance between them, to stop the heat that was already smoldering. Alec looked down at her, his eyes dark and hooded, and pulled her just the tiniest bit closer. She briefly considered pulling away, then quickly decided against it. Alec's body seemed to relax, and she realized that he had been worried she would do just that.

"You're beautiful." His voice was rough, like he hadn't used it in some time, and she tilted her head up to look at him again, to ask him if something was wrong. Her breath left her in a rush at the look in his eyes, at the heat and desire so clear in the dark depths. She expected him to look away, to pull away, to say something, but he just kept looking down at her as he eased her even closer, their bodies pressed again each other.

"Alec—"

He shook his head, stopping her before she could even think of what she should say. Her pulse hammered in her throat as he continued watching her, his eyes hypnotizing, drawing her in, drawing her closer as the plaintive lyrics and soft music wrapped around them.

Alec flattened her hand against his chest, directly over his heart, and she could feel the steady beat racing beneath her palm. The heat from his body seeped into her, warming her. "I'm sorry I never took you dancing. I'm sorry for a lot of things."

AJ lowered her gaze away and stared at his chest, at his hand covering hers, and she wondered if he could feel her fingers trembling. All she wanted was to wrap her arms around him, to lift her face to his for a kiss. But she couldn't. He was no longer hers; she didn't know if he ever had been hers.

She closed her eyes and followed the sway of his body as the heat between them intensified. She should pull away, she knew she should, before he completely consumed her.

AJ opened her eyes and looked up at him, but the words died on her tongue before she could even open her mouth. Alec's face was mere inches away, his gaze searing, demanding as the strains of the chorus grew around them. She lifted her face to his, felt herself reaching for him as he lowered his mouth slowly toward her. He was going to kiss her, she knew it with every molecule of her being, and she was helpless to stop him.

She didn't want to stop him.

Her eyes slowly drifted closed, waiting, both anticipating and dreading the touch of his mouth against hers.

"Alec!"

AJ's body went rigid at the whiny shriek, and she opened her eyes, startled at the noise but not surprised to see Alec's date standing less than a foot away, her face contorted in anger and frustration. One clawed hand reached out and closed over Alec's arm, trying to jerk him toward her.

AJ was slightly surprised when Alec's hold on her tightened, as if he was trying to keep her close. She shook her head and pulled away, not understanding what he was trying to do, if he was playing a game or not. It didn't matter, because she refused to let herself get drawn into it.

Never mind that she had very nearly done just that.

She took a deep breath and stepped away as the song died, and offered Alec a smile that felt forced and faked. "Thanks for the dance, Kolchak. I, um, think your girlfriend wants you."

"AJ..."

She turned and walked away, not caring to hear whatever he had been planning on saying, not wanting to see him touch or hold or even talk to his new girlfriend after he had so easily held her in his arms.

Ian was waiting for her at the edge of the dance floor, a glass of wine held out to her, a look of concern on his face. "Are you okay?"

She took the wine and nearly drained it in one swallow, then gave Ian a wavering smile. "Never better. Is it almost time to leave for the awards ceremony?"

"Yeah, whenever you're ready." Ian watched her for a few long seconds, then nodded and grabbed her hand. AJ was grateful for the comforting touch, even more grateful that Ian chose not to say anything about the foolish dance as he led her through the thinning crowd and outside to the waiting limo.

#

The lights in the ballroom dimmed as the wait staff cleared the last remnants of dinner from the tables. The occupants in the room seemed to sigh in relief all at once, and Alec was no exception. He glanced down at his watch and shifted in the hard chair, wondering why these things were always so drawn out.

He leaned across the table for the pot of coffee that had been placed there. Not that he wanted any of the cold stuff, but it gave him something to do. He poured the coffee as slow as possible, then offered it to everyone else at the table.

Of course, nobody was really paying him any attention, so it didn't surprise him when there were no takers. He slammed the pot down on the table more forcefully than he had planned. Two of his teammates at the table turned and shot him a look of impatience, letting him know that he was still on their shit list, even though he had shown up to the ceremony by himself.

If he had been smart, he would have shown up at the pre-party by himself, as well. But he hadn't, and he was very much afraid that it was too late to make things right. The look in AJ's eyes...the mix of hurt and loss when Brandi tried pulling him away from her would stay with him for a long time. Seeing AJ leave with Ian had pushed him over the edge. He dragged Brandi out of the club minutes later and rushed to get her back to her place, dropping her off with the barest of apologies.

And a plea that she never bother him again. He left before she could make a scene and rushed to the ceremony, hoping for a chance to speak with AJ before it got started.

But he was too late.

He glanced at the table just in front and off to the side of his, the table where Ian was sitting with AJ and a few other teammates and their dates. Everyone was smiling, free of the tension that hung over Alec's own table. Ian had his arm draped casually along the back of AJ's chair and he leaned down to say something, causing her to laugh. Alec clenched his jaw and looked at the empty chair next to him, knowing that AJ would be seated with him tonight if he hadn't so thoroughly screwed things up.

"Shit." Alec snapped the word under his breath and pushed back his chair hard enough that people turned to stare at him. He didn't bother apologizing, just turned and stormed in the direction of the bar as the room broke into a spattering of applause when the emcee approached the microphone.

Alec returned to the table several minutes later with a full bottle of wine that he placed in front of him with a loud thud. He ignored the verbal admonishments from those around him and poured himself a glass, then pushed his chair away from the table, distancing himself even more.

The ceremony dragged on, the restlessness of the crowd broken only by the humor of the emcee. Alec glanced down at his watch again, then let his gaze wander over the room. More than half of the players in attendance were beginning to fidget in their chairs, and Alec knew from experience that the next hour would be the longest of the night. Whoever had the bright idea to confine Baltimore's most athletic figures to a four-hour awards ceremony didn't understand athletes very well.

Alec let his gaze travel to AJ's table again, telling himself that he wasn't spying. He just wanted to look at her, at how beautiful she was. And he was just curious and wanted to see if AJ was having fun.

Because it certainly looked like she had been having fun all night, both at the pre-party, and even here at the stuffy ceremony. He didn't want to admit that she and Ian looked good together, and he really didn't want to accept the fact that they were dating. He hoped that tonight was just a favor, nothing more.

Because he really didn't know what he would do if they really *were* dating. And he was a complete hypocrite, a fool. He had no rights, no claims, where AJ was concerned. There had been at least a dozen different things he could have done to change that, but he hadn't. Instead, he gave in to spite and let everyone think that he had reunited with a one-time ex-girlfriend. Including Brandi.

Yeah, he was a hypocrite. Worse, even.

He studied the table in front of him, his eyes narrowing on the two empty seats where Ian and AJ had been sitting. How could he have missed them leaving? Which didn't make sense. Why would they have left? Alec knew that AJ was supposed to be doing a story on the awards; she wouldn't have just left.

He glanced around the room, trying to be nonchalant at first, then being just downright obvious about it when he couldn't see them anywhere. His gut twisted at the thoughts that came to mind. Was AJ really interested in Ian? Had they left to go somewhere more private?

No. Despite the bitter acid in his stomach that image brought, Alec knew better. AJ wasn't like that. And if he was honest, he knew that Ian wasn't like that either.

He shifted so he could see the rear of the room better, his gaze drifting over the few people stopped at the bar, searching. The only familiar face he saw was that of the slime ball weasel that used to work at AJ's paper. What was his name? Gordon, Jerome...Gerry. That was it, Gerry Brown. Why was he slinking around the back with a photographer? Alec didn't want to know, and didn't really care.

He turned back around to face the front, clapping automatically when a couple of his teammates were awarded for their efforts with some local charities. The team itself had received an award for its fundraising efforts on behalf of children's cancer studies, and Alec stood with the rest of the Banners to applaud as Sonny and the GM went on stage to accept the award.

He was getting ready to take his seat when a hand closed around his arm. Alec turned around, not sure what to expect, and was surprised to come face-to-face with a worried-looking Ian. He leaned closer, keeping his voice low.

"Something's wrong with AJ."

Alec straightened and searched the crowd, looking for her, then faced Ian. "What's wrong? Where is she?"

Ian motioned for him to follow, leading the way toward the lobby of the banquet hall. "I don't know what's wrong. She started feeling bad about an hour ago, then asked for help to get to the ladies' room. Something about her head. Alec, she was stumbling and acting like she was drunk, but she hasn't had anything to drink since leaving the pre-party."

"Her head? Shit. Where is she now?"

"In the ladies' room." They made their way through the last of the tables and were approaching the foyer leading to the lobby when Ian stopped. "Alec, that dick wad reporter is hanging around waiting. I think he saw us go in there."

Alec clenched his jaw and looked around. Sure enough, the guy was pacing back and forth, muttering to himself as he punched at his phone. The photographer Alec had seen earlier was nowhere in sight.

He motioned to Ian, then strode purposefully through the lobby and straight into the ladies' room as if they had every right to go in there. He stopped as soon as the door closed, his heart squeezing painfully when his eyes rested on AJ.

She was curled up in the upholstered chair, her hands wrapped around her head, her fingers digging into her temples. A small whimper escaped her and he watched as she tried to raise her head, her eyes slow to focus. He closed the distance and knelt in front of her, closing his hands over hers, careful not to jostle her. He kept his voice as low as possible. "Do you have your medicine?"

She shook her head, the tiniest of movements that he knew caused her pain. He let out a sigh then turned to Ian and motioned him closer. "Ian, find some medicine. The strongest you can find.

Somebody out there has to have some prescription ibuprofen at the least."

"What is it? What's wrong with her?"

"A migraine. And a really bad one from the looks of it."

"A migraine? You mean, like a headache?"

"It's a bit worse than that. Now go." Alec shifted, wondering what he could do. He released her hands and walked over to the marble vanity, grabbing some heavy paper linen towels and soaking them under cold water. He squeezed the water out, then returned to AJ. As gently as he could, he moved her, settling her on his lap and holding the wet cloths over her eyes. Her hands squeezed over his, holding the cloth in place as her head rolled against his chest.

The door banged open and a soft whimper escaped AJ as Ian rushed in. Alec tossed him a look and motioned with his head, signaling for quiet. Ian walked over, holding out a glass of water and a large white pill.

"Eight hundred milligram ibuprofen. Will this work?"

"Better than nothing." Alec straightened, supporting AJ as he took the pill from Ian and helped her take it. A shudder racked her body as she sipped the water, and she settled back against him with a whimper.

"Ian, I need to get her home, but I can't drive her in my truck. Can you—"

"I'll have the driver bring the limo around then make sure your truck makes it home. But there's a problem."

"What?"

"The dick wad is starting to make noise and attract attention, and he's got a photographer with him. I heard him say something about...he was pretty loud and accusing certain reporters of acting like drunken, uh, um, sluts."

Alec clenched his jaw and fought the urge to go back out and use the idiot for boxing practice. He looked down, surprised when AJ whispered his name, surprised to see her eyes trying to focus on him.

"Don't." The word was uttered so softly it couldn't even be called a whisper. Alec sighed and dropped a kiss on the top of her head, then cradled her closer as her eyes fluttered shut.

"Ian, I need a distraction. Something to keep him so occupied he won't notice when we leave." Ian nodded and hurried out, leaving them alone. Alec stared down at AJ, curled so trustingly against him, pain digging at the now-pale features of her face. His heart squeezed painfully, and he instinctively tightened his hold around her. Another whimper escaped her, causing his heart to turn over.

"AJ, can you wrap your arms around my neck? It'll be easier to carry—"

"No."

"AJ, don't be—"

"Your...award..."

Alec's heart constricted at her words. She was in his arms, curled against him in pain, and her only thought was of the stupid award he was supposed to get. He bit back a bitter laugh and dropped another kiss on the top of her head. "AJ, I don't give a damn about any award. All I care about is you. They can give me all the awards in the world and none of it matters if I don't have you."

Her hands twisted more tightly in the lapels of his jacket as she murmured something against his chest. He couldn't make out the words, but he didn't need to, not when her eyes fluttered open and looked into his. He swallowed against the raw emotion burning his throat but didn't look away. He didn't even blink, for fear that she wouldn't see what was burning in his own eyes.

"I love you, AJ. Without you, nothing else matters."

Her eyes drifted shut and her lips moved, but he couldn't make out what she was saying. Her head rolled against his chest and he realized the migraine was too much for her, that she was giving into it. Blinking against the burning in his eyes, he stood up slowly, cradling her as gently as possible as he made his way to the door.

There was a sudden commotion on the other side of the door, and Alec knew that Ian had conjured up his needed distraction. But what he saw when he opened the door was enough to actually make him stop in complete surprise.

"Holy shit, Ian." It took real effort for Alec to mutter the words under his breath instead of shouting them. Ian's idea of a distraction was going to end with him getting beaten to a pulp: the fool was in the face of one of the defensive lineman from the football team, the one who had danced several times with AJ earlier. Ian was arguing with him and shoving his finger into a chest the size of a refrigerator. The lineman wasn't budging. Worse, there was a crowd forming, and Ian was quickly becoming outnumbered.

As a distraction, it was working. But Alec didn't want to think about the outcome. He shook his head and hoped his friend knew what he was doing, then tightened his hold on AJ and carried her toward the exit.

He pushed through the door without being stopped, thankful that Ian's limo was at the curb, waiting with the door open. Alec eased into the back of the limo and settled in the lush seat with AJ collapsed against him, an agonized sob rushing from her as another shudder racked her body. He wrapped his arms around her and rubbed her temples, murmuring soft words as the limo pulled away.

EIGHTEEN

The movement was tentative, slow, but enough to pull Alec from his light doze. His arms tightened automatically, not willing to let go.

"How are you feeling?" His voice was a rough whisper in the darkness of the room, and he felt AJ's body tense for a long moment. She finally relaxed against him, but not as completely as before.

"Tired. Like I've been run over." Her voice was raspy, a hot breath against his chest.

He reached up and stroked her hair, brushing it behind her ear before gently massaging her temple. Thoughts of their very first night together rushed to his memory, of him holding her in sleep, of easing her pain as another migraine seized her. Thoughts of all the other nights since then, of how she curled up against him in her sleep.

Much like she was now.

Alec took a deep breath and continued stroking her hair, fighting the memories, fighting the regrets of the last couple of weeks. "Close your eyes, relax. Go back to sleep."

He felt her begin to shake her head, heard her soft moan. "No, I can't." Her hand reached up and closed around his, and for one brief second, Alec thought she was going to hold it. Instead, she moved his hand away from her; he could feel her shift, and knew she was pushing herself up on her elbow. Pushing herself away from him.

"I need to go home."

Alec swallowed his sigh of frustration, knowing it wouldn't

help. "AJ, you don't need to go home. It's the middle of the night, it's been a long night. Lie back down and go to sleep, let your body rest and heal."

He held his breath, waiting, hoping. AJ's body was still tense against him and he felt her shift in the darkness. Was she getting up? He released his hold on her and waited some more, then sighed when she moved away from him.

But she didn't get up. She rolled over onto her back and shifted away from him. There were only inches separating them, but she might as well have been in the next room for as distant as she seemed. Her body was little more than a shadow in the dark room, and Alec wished there was more light so he could see her face more clearly.

"I shouldn't be here."

It wasn't much of an opening, but Alec jumped on it. He rolled over and propped himself on his elbow then looked down at her, reaching out tentatively with his left hand and letting it rest gently on her arm. "Yes, you should. You belong here."

Her arm tensed under his touch but she didn't move it away, and she didn't say anything. He felt her relax, and he shifted just the tiniest bit closer, running his hand slowly up and down her arm. Quiet minutes went by, and he thought she might have fallen asleep again.

Alec lowered his head to the pillow, just inches from her, and eased even closer, their bodies barely touching. He trailed his hand down her arm and wrapped his fingers around hers, content to be next to her, willing to settle for just this tiniest of touches.

"Where's your girlfriend?" The question was soft, barely a ragged whisper. Alec stilled, not so much because of the question itself, but because of the sound of AJ's voice. He was suddenly grateful for the darkness, because he was very much afraid that she was crying—or rather, trying not to cry—and he didn't think he could handle seeing that.

So he squeezed her fingers, closed his eyes, and answered honestly. "She's right here next to me, where she belongs."

There was a short laugh, obviously forced, as AJ pulled her hand from his. "Wow, Kolchak, funny. I meant your current girlfriend. The one you took to the ball."

She shifted away from him and Alec knew she was going to

get up, that she was going to leave his bed. It didn't matter that she had no way to get anywhere, she was still going to leave. He moved, rolling over and closing his arms around her, his face inches from hers.

"AJ, you are the only one who matters to me. You. Nobody else. Brandi was...she was a stupid mistake two years ago, and a stupid mistake two weeks ago. Nothing happened between us, and she means nothing to me. She never did." He paused, swallowing, and lowered his head even closer to her. "Do you remember what I told you earlier tonight?"

"Alec, don't."

"'Don't' what?"

"Alec, please, I just...I need to leave. I need to go home." Her body was tense in his hold, but she made no attempt to move. From this close, he could see her eyes were closed. Her voice was strained, as if she was forcing the words through a sore throat. He swallowed hard, and without wanting to, he reached out and ran his hand across one soft cheek.

His fingers touched the dampness there, and she tensed again and tried to pull away, a groan of frustration escaping her. His own stomach clenched as a wave of regret and sorrow washed over him, weighing him down. He rested his forehead against hers, swallowing back his own emotion at the evidence of her tears.

"AJ, I love you. And I am so sorry. For everything. I never meant..." He took a deep breath and let it out. "I am the world's biggest ass. And I wouldn't blame you if you never spoke to me again. But—"

"Alec, stop." AJ shifted beneath him and tried to turn her face away, but he held it in place with a gentle hand against her still-damp cheek.

"Listen to me, please." She finally stopped trying to turn away from him, but her body remained tense. He took a deep breath and let the words come out in a rush, not knowing how long he might have before she really pushed him away.

If she hadn't already, in the way that meant the most.

"I'm sorry I acted like an ass from the very beginning. And I'm sorry that I never told you how I feel. I'm sorry that the one and only time I ever took you out, it was to a strip club. I'm sorry that I treated you like one of the guys and I'm sorry for not making you feel special. And I am so sorry that when Brandi first showed up at the rink, I tried to laugh it off. It didn't mean anything to me, and I never even stopped to think what it meant to you. I—"

"You humiliated me, Alec. Worse than that, you hurt me."

Her softly spoken words made him pause. Of all the emotions he might have expected, humiliation had never crossed his mind. He pulled back just a little and looked down into her face, realized that her eyes were open and staring over his shoulder. He had no idea what to say, and was saved from saying the wrong thing when she spoke again.

"All that other stuff...doesn't matter. But that day at the rink... You thought so little of me that you let me go as soon as she came up to you. She pushed me away and you let her. If it hadn't been for Ian, I would have fallen flat on my face. It's a moment in time frozen for prosperity forever. I know, because the pictures—the ones that didn't make it into the paper—were sent to me."

"AJ, I didn't—"

"Yeah, I know, you didn't mean to. She caught you off guard. I get that. But right after that? You disappeared. And then...you laughed about it. Like it was some big joke. No big deal. You have no idea...how much...that hurt." She paused, took several deep breaths, and Alec knew she was doing her best to keep him from seeing her tears. But he did see them, and it was tearing him apart inside. "And then, I start seeing pictures of you two together, and all I kept hearing is how the two of you are back together. Real funny...considering how you told me...she was nothing. And you have no...idea how much...that hurt."

"Yes, I do. Because if it's anything like how I felt when I saw you with Ian yesterday...if I made you feel even a little bit like how I felt, then yes, I do. And God, I am so sorry, AJ. So sorry." He held his breath, waiting, then, slowly, he lowered his face and touched his lips against hers, the barest of brushes. He trailed his lips across her cheek, tasting the saltiness of her tears, feeling her anger and pain.

"AJ, I am so sorry. For so many things, but most of all for hurting you. And I don't know what to say, I don't know how else to tell you what I'm feeling. But it's tearing me apart seeing you like this, knowing that it's all my fault. Please..." Alec paused, swallowing against the lump in his throat, not knowing what he was asking for, struggling for the right thing to say, struggling for the right thing to do.

AJ finally turned her head and looked up at him, her eyes shining in the darkness. He swallowed again as their gazes met, as he saw a mix of emotions swirling in the blue depths of her beautiful eyes. The moment hung between them, suspended, and it felt like they were waiting. For what, he didn't know.

Finally, afraid it was the wrong thing to do, afraid it would push her away forever, he dipped his head towards hers, his lips closing over hers in a tentative kiss. She didn't turn her head, didn't pull away, so he gradually, hesitantly deepened the kiss. Her mouth opened on a soft sigh and he seized the opportunity, swept his tongue into the soft darkness of her mouth, exploring, claiming.

Her body relaxed under his, and she reached up and ran one hand through his hair, then down along his neck and shoulder. He waited, afraid she would push him away, then groaned when she pulled him closer, her tongue darting out and dancing with his.

His kiss became more urgent, his touch almost desperate as he shifted, moving his body over hers, trying to show her what he couldn't put into words. He pulled back, afraid of going too fast, of pushing her. Alec didn't want there to be any regrets in the morning, he wanted her to be sure before he went any further.

But when he pulled back, she reached for him. When he tried to speak, she crushed her mouth against his and robbed him of speech. And when she wrapped her legs around his waist and thrust her hips against his, he lost control of all thought except how to show her that she belonged with him, that he belonged with her.

That they belonged together.

#

The phone vibrated again, skipping across the surface of the desk. AJ gritted her teeth and tried to ignore it, then grabbed it and tossed it across the cubicle. The phone hit the bulletin board hanging on the fabric wall, bounced off, and clattered to the floor. The battery popped out and bounced across the tiled surface, coming to a stop near her feet. She grunted and kicked it away, then laid her head down on the desk with a frustrated sigh.

Several minutes later, the extension in her little office began ringing. With a muttered curse, she lifted her head and stared at the phone, her jaw clenching when she saw the number on the Caller ID readout. She reached out and yanked the cord from the base, silencing it.

AJ wondered if it would work, but didn't dare get her hopes up. Every phone around her had been ringing nonstop for the last two days.

Since she had spent the night with Alec.

Since she had slept with Alec.

Since Alec had told her he loved her.

But it was a mistake. It had to be. He did not love her. He couldn't love her, not when he had just been seeing his old girlfriend. She believed him when he told her that nothing had happened between them, but she couldn't believe he loved her. It was a mistake, emotion born out of guilt.

She had tried telling him that, but he refused to believe her. And he kept calling. And calling.

AJ laid her head back on the desk, wondering if it would help if she banged her head against the hard surface. She sensed a shadow cross over her, confirmed by a rough clearing of the throat followed by the impatient rustle of paper.

She didn't need to look up to know it was Tim.

"How's that article coming?"

"What? The one on the little league team? I just emailed it to you." Yeah, that had been a rough one that had really stretched the limits of her abilities. She briefly wondered if he was here to give her another hard-hitting assignment, something even more far-fetched and worse as punishment.

He grunted, and she heard more rustling. "I still love this headline: 'Baltimore Ball, Baltimore Brawl'. Catchy, don't you think? Great story, too."

She flinched when the paper hit her in the head and she looked up, her gaze sweeping across the bold head line. "Tim, I said I screwed up. I know I did. How many times do I have to say I'm sorry? How long do I have to grovel?" She looked from Sunday's paper to her editor.

Or maybe it was soon-to-be ex-editor. Getting fired would fit perfectly into the mess she had gotten herself into. One night. That was all it had taken for her to plummet into the bowels of hell.

If not for the pain and anger still simmering inside her, she may have been able to find some twisted humor in the situation. Especially since, when you got to the bottom of it, the entire thing was her fault. If she hadn't had the migraine...

Alec wouldn't have tried to save her.

Ian wouldn't have created a distraction.

She wouldn't have gone home with Alec.

There wouldn't have been a huge fight between players from three of Baltimore's sports teams.

She wouldn't have slept with Alec.

Alec wouldn't have told her he loved her.

AJ swallowed a groan and put her head back on the desk, unable to look at Tim when he fired her. She deserved it. She knew she did. He had gone out of his way for her, showed his trust and belief in her and got her the job she had wanted for years.

Yet she couldn't even cover a plain, simple awards ceremony. Yeah, she was sharp and talented alright.

"AJ, you're disappointing me."

The plainly spoken words fell over her like ice water, shocking, sobering. She swallowed and nodded her head, waiting for his next words, knowing she was getting fired.

"You would have never put up with this a month ago. Where did all your fight go?"

She raised her head and stared at Tim in confusion. "What?"

"You heard me. A month ago you would have hit me with so much attitude over an assignment like the little league one. Now you just roll over and give in. I'm disappointed."

Her mouth opened, then snapped shut as she tried to figure out what to say. "But...Tim, I screwed it up and—"

"Yeah, you did. So suck it up and move on."

"But...Tim, it was my fault. The whole thing."

He took two steps toward her and rested his hip against her desk, staring down at her with calm eyes. "You said you had a migraine. You got sick. Even I can't blame you for that."

"But..." AJ lowered her gaze to the newspaper on the desk and took a deep breath, then gave Tim all the details, starting with the onset of her migraine and ending with Alec taking her home. She didn't say whose home, but the look on Tim's face let her know she didn't have to. And then...he started laughing. A small chuckle that quickly grew into a hearty belly laugh.

AJ pushed away from her desk and stared up at him, wondering if he had finally lost it. Because she didn't find anything remotely funny about the situation.

Several minutes went by before Tim stopped laughing. "That would have been something to see. And it also explains a lot. Well, you'll be glad to hear you have a chance at redemption. A press conference is scheduled at the practice facilities in one hour, and you were specifically requested. I just got the call."

"Me? Why?"

"No idea. But don't look a gift horse in the mouth. Like I said: redemption."

"Tim, I can't. Somebody else has to do it." Redemption or not, she could not see Alec again. Not after what happened. But Tim obviously didn't care. All traces of his earlier laughter were gone. His face was a blank mask as he leaned toward her.

"Would you care to tell me why?"

AJ looked up at him for only a second, then lowered her gaze to her folded hands. She couldn't tell him.

She couldn't *not* tell him.

"Because..." She paused, took a deep breath and let it out. "Because Alec told me he loved me. And...I'm pretty sure I love him."

Long silence greeted her statement. She finally looked up at Tim, waiting for him to say something, expecting...well, if not sympathy, at least understanding.

"This is a problem why?"

"Because..." She trailed off and shook her head. How could she put it into words to make him understand? Said out loud, her reasons sounded weak, foolish. "Because..."

Tim cut her off with a short wave of his hand and pushed away from her desk with a disgusted sigh. "Whatever the problem is, it's all yours. Deal with it." He walked to the entrance of the cubicle then turned and looked at her, his face impassive, his eyes distant. "But a word of advice, AJ. If you don't get over to that rink, you're risking something a lot more important than just a job."

NINETEEN

The door closed and latched with a thud, leaving AJ with the uncomfortable feeling of being entombed in a large cavern. That feeling grew stronger when she realized that the rink seemed deserted.

She walked further inside, her eyes adjusting to the dim light after being in the sun, and made her way to the interior hall leading to the offices. Noise from the other end of the rink caught her attention and she paused, turning to look toward the far end zone.

There, gathered around the net, stood a handful of players. AJ frowned, then turned back around and reached for the doorknob, wondering what was going on when the door wouldn't open.

"Hey Johnson! Over here!"

AJ turned back to face the ice, still frowning. That had sounded suspiciously like Alec's voice...but different. She glanced at her watch, wondering if she had missed the press conference. Or if she was too early. But no, according to the time, the press conference was supposed to start in a few minutes.

So where was everyone?

"Johnson, over here!"

AJ squinted, trying to make out the faces in the distance, but couldn't see clearly enough. She glanced back at the locked door then shrugged and headed toward the ice, walking around the edge of the boards toward the player's bench. Her steps faltered as she got closer, her eyes widening in disbelief.

Several players were gathered around the net, huddled

together as...

She stopped and blinked, not believing what she was seeing. She had to be hallucinating. She stepped closer to the boards, staring at the sight of Alec in the net.

Literally...in the net. It looked like he was tied to the posts. Upside down. Her gaze momentarily got stuck on the sight of all his tanned, muscled flesh before she realized...

Yes, he really was hanging upside down in the net. And he was wearing nothing but gym shorts, a pair of skates, and his catching glove.

AJ blinked again and looked even closer, her mouth opening and closing silently. Ian broke away from the group of players clustered around Alec and skated over to her, a grin on his face. She swallowed a gasp when he stopped less than a foot away and winced at the bruises she saw on his face. He waved away her concern and motioned to the player's bench.

"There's a pair of skates ready for you. Put 'em on and get out here."

"Uh, Ian. Why is Alec upside down in the net?"

Ian looked toward the end zone, then back at her and shrugged. "No reason. Just a little bet. C'mon, get out here."

"Ian—"

"Hey Johnson, will you hurry up?"

She turned away from Ian and stared at Alec, still swinging upside down. Even from this distance she could see the goose bumps along his skin, and noticed that his face was starting to turn a nice shade of red.

"Alec, what are you doing?"

"Oh, just hanging around, waiting on you."

She bit back a laughing groan at his words and walked into the player's box, not knowing what to do. Should she call someone? Or should she just wait to see what happened next?

Once she had her skates laced up, Ian opened the door for her and she drifted out onto the ice, easing closer to the net and leaning sideways to get a better look at Alec. He offered her a small smile and a little wave, and she still didn't know whether she should be laughing or calling for help.

"So I take it there's no press conference?"

"That was my idea." Ian slid to a stop next to her, spraying ice onto Alec, grinning at his swift intake of breath. "I figured that was the best way to get you down here."

AJ stared at him for a few long seconds, waiting for more explanation. When he offered none, she glanced around at the other players—including Randy and Jean-Pierre—and noticed that all of them were sporting assorted cuts and bruises on their hands and faces from the "Baltimore Brawl". In fact, Alec was the only one unmarred. She cast another quick look at Alec then stepped closer to Ian, her arms crossed, her expression serious.

"Ian, what's going on?"

"Did you ever see that ice hockey movie with all the kids?" At her hesitant nod, he continued. "Do you remember how they got the goalie used to the pucks coming at him? They tied him up in the net and just let them fly. We're going to do the same thing to Alec."

"Uh..." AJ paused, not sure what to think. He couldn't be serious. Could he? "But Alec's upside down. In nothing but shorts. Besides, he's already a good goalie. So I don't get—"

Jean-Pierre interrupted her, a charming smile on his rugged face. "It's not to make him a good goalie, eh? This is for the other night, for what he did and what he got away with."

"What he did...What?" AJ practically screamed the last word, mortified as realization sunk in. They were really going to pellet him with pucks because of what happened between Alec and her? She gazed at the serious faces around her, then looked back at Ian, deciding he was the most reasonable. "Ian, you can't do this. You were there, you know what happened. Alec didn't—"

"Sorry AJ. But we know how Alec treated you and that he's an ass. It's the least he deserves, especially since he didn't even stand up for you Saturday night when the fight broke out."

"That's because he was too busy taking care of—" AJ snapped her mouth closed and stared at Ian. He looked back at her in wide-eyed innocence, with not even a hint of a smile on his face. She narrowed her eyes at him. Ian knew exactly where Alec was when the fight broke out.

She crossed her arms and stared at Ian for another long second, then turned and stared at Alec. He was still hanging from the net by his legs, watching her closely. She ignored the warm look in his eyes and the sight of all that bare flesh and turned back to Ian. "Okay, you say he deserves it. You're right, he does. So now what?"

A strangled groan came from Alec but she ignored it, watching as the hockey players glanced at each other, obviously not expecting her to agree so quickly. Ian shuffled his feet, glanced behind her at Alec, then shrugged and offered her his stick. "Well, I guess you go first."

There was another strangled groan from behind her, followed by shuffling and banging. AJ continued to ignore Alec and reached out for Ian's stick, only to have him pull it out of her reach when he glanced behind her. "That is, unless Alec can really show us he's sorry for being such an ass and that he didn't mean to treat you the way he did. I mean, he did tell us that he loved you, and that he even told you he loved you, but that you wouldn't listen to him." Ian paused, a worried look crossing his face as he skated backwards a few feet. AJ watched him in confusion, wondering why he and the other guys were slowly backing up.

But he kept talking, glancing behind her as he drifted a few feet further away. "Of course, I don't believe that for a second because if he did tell you he loved you, you would listen to him and—"

"Donovan, you completely screwed that up."

AJ jumped at the voice directly behind her then turned and would have fallen on the ice if Alec's strong arms hadn't caught her. She instinctively grabbed his shoulders, her hands clenching against his chilled flesh as he looked down at her, heat in his eyes.

"AJ, I love you. What Ian was trying to say is—I screwed up. Big time screwed up. And I'm sorry. I was hoping that you'd come here and see this, and take pity on me. That you'd realize I really do love you and that I really am sorry—"

AJ leaned forward and pressed her lips to his, effectively silencing him. His arms wrapped more tightly around her, pulling her so close that the chill of his flesh seeped through the sweater she was wearing. She broke the kiss with a sigh and pulled away only slightly, keeping her arms wrapped around his neck. "How can I not love someone who goes to such a drastic extreme to say he's sorry?"

His eyes darkened as he gazed down at her, and she could see him swallowing hard. "I'm really hoping that means you love me. You have no idea how much I'm hoping that."

She smiled and leaned forward to kiss him again, just the barest brushing of their lips. "I love you Alec. With all of me."

His arms tightened around her, lifting her off the ice as his mouth closed over hers in a searing kiss. It was too easy to get lost in his touch, too easy to get lost in the raw emotion swirling around them. AJ pulled back, motioning for him to let her down, then smiled up at the confused look in his eyes.

"So, Kolchak, how about a bet?"

He stared at her, his brows raised in surprise. "A bet?"

"Yeah, a bet. Kinda like the last one."

"A bet?" He repeated. He loosened his hold around her and stepped back, his mouth twitching upwards in a small grin. "Okay. What's the bet?"

AJ looked behind her, not surprised to see they still had company. She motioned for Ian to come closer, then grabbed the stick from his hand when he stopped next to her. She looked back at Alec and smiled. "I score, and you have to put up with me for 24/7."

Alec watched her, heat simmering in his eyes, then shook his head. "That doesn't work for me. How about...if you score, you get my heart. Forever."

Her heart stuttered then kick-started into overdrive at the emotion in Alec's voice. She blinked, hard, against the sudden burning in her eyes and opened her mouth to say something when a puck was dropped on the ice in front of her. She looked down at the rubber slab, then up to see Alec drifting back to the net.

And suddenly, what had seemed like a light-hearted joke just minutes ago turned into a serious challenge that filled her with anxiety and desperation. "Alec, I love you. I was only joking. This is silly—"

"One shot, AJ. Cross the line and you win. My heart. Forever."

"Alec..." She paused and cleared her throat, surprised at the nervousness that made her tremble.

"C'mon AJ, one shot. Cross the line."

She glanced down at the puck, then up at Alec standing in the net just a few feet away. Wearing nothing but shorts, skates, and his catching glove. She could do this. She could.

Biting back a nervous laugh, she placed the blade of the stick against the puck and pushed off with her skates, then pulled back and shot. She was less than three feet away, there was no way she could miss.

She watched the puck lob toward the net, biting back a smile as it prepared to sail past Alec...who leaned to the side and caught it with almost no effort.

AJ sucked in her breath with a hiss, her heart literally stopping as she Alec pulled the glove closer to his chest. What had just happened? Did this mean...but it couldn't! She loved him. And he told her he loved her. How could he—

"AJ!"

She looked up, startled at her name being called so loudly, and realized that Alec had been trying to get her attention before. He raised one brow at her, then crooked his finger in a motion for her to come closer. She hung her head and drifted forward, willing the burning in her eyes to stop.

"AJ, look at me. No, don't shake your head. Look at me."

She swallowed and blinked, then raised her head, refusing to do anything that would make this worse. Alec's warm gaze drifted over her, searching, before a smile broke across his face. She watched, stunned, as he tossed the puck behind him into the net before reaching for her and wrapping her tightly in his hold.

"You always had it, AJ. My heart. You had it from the minute you made that first bet. I just didn't realize it, and when I did, I didn't know how to tell you. But I'm telling you now—I love you. No matter what happens. Forever."

"Oh, Alec." She paused, blinking again, but not really caring if he saw the tears this time, because they were tears of happiness. "I love you, Alec. I always will. Even if you are going to get frostbite from being stubborn and half-naked—"

He stopped her with a kiss, a deep one that left her breathless when he pulled away. "Say it again."

She looked into his eyes, at the clear emotion in their dark depths, and felt heat blossom through her. "I love you Alec."

He smiled, then claimed her mouth in a searing kiss that had the other players wondering how long it would be before the couple melted the ice under them.

But the two of them didn't care, because they had both made the biggest bet of their lives.

And came out winners in the most important game of all.

CROSSING THE LINE

About the Author

Lisa grew up with an overactive imagination, strong encouragement from her parents, and an insatiable infatuation with the Peanuts gang. That infatuation—along with an impatience she has yet to outgrow—jump-started her love of writing. After all, why should she be forced to wait a whole week to read the stories of her favorite characters when she could create stories for them whenever she wanted?

That love of writing continued to grow, along with all those voices in her head, even during her assorted careers: first as a firefighter with the Baltimore County Fire Department, then a very brief (and not very successful) stint at bartending in east Baltimore, and finally as the Director of Retail Operations for a busy Civil War non-profit.

Lisa currently lives in Maryland with her husband and two sons, one very spoiled Border Collie, two cats with major attitude, several head of cattle, and entirely too many chickens to count.

Please visit her website www.LisaBKamps.com for exciting information on new releases, to subscribe to her newsletter, and just general craziness.

You may also follow Lisa on Twitter @LBKamps, find her on Facebook at https://www.facebook.com/LisaBKamps or reach her via email at LisaBKamps@gmail.com

Forensics accountant Bobbi Reeves is pulled back into a world of shadows in order to go undercover as a personal assistant with the Baltimore Banners. Her assignment: get close to defenseman Nikolai Petrovich and uncover the reason he's being extorted. But she doesn't expect the irrational attraction she feels—or the difficulty in helping someone who doesn't want it.

Nikolai Petrovich, a veteran defenseman for the Banners, has no need for a personal assistant—especially not one hired by the team. During the last eight years, he has learned to live simply...and alone. Experience has taught him that letting people close puts them in danger. He doesn't want a personal assistant, and he certainly doesn't need anyone prying into his personal life. But that doesn't stop his physical reaction to the unusual woman assigned to him.

They are drawn together in spite of their differences, and discover a heated passion that neither expected. But when the game is over, will the secrets they keep pull them closer together...or tear them apart?

Kayli Evans lives a simple life, handling the daily operations of her small family farm and acting as the primary care-taker for her fourteen-year-old niece. She knows the importance of enjoying each minute, of living life to its fullest. But she still has worries: about her older brother's safety in the military, about the rift between her two brothers, and about her niece's security and making ends meet. And now there's a new worry she doesn't want: Ian Donovan, her brother's friend.

Ian is a carefree hockey player for the Baltimore Banners who has relatively few worries—until he finds himself suddenly babysitting his seven-year-old nieces for an extended period of time. He has no idea what he's doing, and is thrust even further into the unknown when he's forced to participate in the twins' newest hobby. Meeting Kayli opens a different world for him, a simpler world where family, trust, and love are what matters most.

CPSIA information can be obtained
at www.ICGtesting.com
Printed in the USA
LVOW12s2316160517
534791LV00002B/145/P